MW01101237

The Third Person

And Other Stories

Zhong Jingjing

pcdq

Publish on Demand Global

This edition was co-published by Publish on Demand Global, LLC.

Translation Funds Granted by China Book International (CBI).

Publish on Demand Global, LLC
12620 FM 1960, Suite A4-507
Houston, TX 77065
www.publishondemandglobal.com

ISBN: 978-1-62516-478-0

Design: Dedicated Book Services (www.netdbs.com)

The Third Person

It happened one day in February and that day was a Thursday. According to the Bible, it was on Thursday that God created the moon, the stars, and the sun, and let them give light unto the earth. God saw that it was good and it was so. So Thursday is a very important day. The very Thursday that I want to talk about, that Thursday in February, is also a very important day to me because on that day, I, a desperate, exiled prisoner, took an incredible action: I ran away with another prisoner named Lao Jian.

This is how it happened: because of a terrible famine spread across the entire country, at the mine located in the depths of the Gobi, where approximately 1,000 exiles were jailed, over 800 had already starved to death. We came from different regions, and were sent there for a variety of reasons. We left our youth, our sweat, and several decades of our lives behind on a land so barren that even birds forsook it. We were both coolies and prisoners, without any freedom. Our daily food ration was just two *liang*, but even this was eventually discontinued, leaving us to eat only the bark of trees. We didn't dare to complain because food was really so scarce that even the guards went hungry. What made it unbearable was that with so little food, we still had to go work in the mines. So when famine struck, we had less chance to survive than those who didn't have to work, and we could do nothing but die unless we became supernatural beings who could live on wind and water. Of course, along with the other dying prisoners I was just an ordinary person who could not survive without food, to enjoy the sun, the stars, and the moon created by the kind-hearted God. So I, along with that guy called Lao Jian, decided to run away, and the day of our departure was set for Thursday.

We decided this after the woman left. She was very weak, yet every few months, she would trek thousands of miles there to visit her husband and bring him some life-saving biscuits. Yet even with her great effort she could not save his life. Her husband, the doctor, died two days before she arrived and he was buried on the sand hill. While she was there, she cried day and night, and the sound travelled heart-breakingly and breathlessly across the Gobi. As it echoed in our ears, we could almost smell the blood in the wind around us, and this made us remember our own wives and parents, so we made up our minds that we would not wait there to die, even if we might become solitary ghosts on the Gobi.

We left at midnight, and I remember clearly the moon, shining so brightly, hanging in the sky, making the sand on the ground look like white snow. This reminded us of *Runtu*, written by Mr. Lu Xun, only the sea was far away, and there were no sleeping watermelons, badgers with sharp hairs, or a young boy with a silver necklace and a javelin at hand. There were only two emaciated, nearly dying prisoners, stubbly-bearded, on the Gobi encircled by endless yellow sand from which it seemed one could never escape. But the two of us had to find a way out, to leave the horrible place where even birds dared not to stay. Were we crazy? How many persons died on this same nightmare-like journey only to be left un-buried? We didn't dare to think about this and we didn't want to think about it, either.

One month before our action, Lao Jian and I began to plot our route. As we were feeding the horses on the farmland, Lao Jian had a peek at a map that belonged to a guard. He told me that if we went east, or north, or west, there were several patrol lines, and it was from these directions that prisoners who tried to escape in the past were recaptured. Therefore, the only pos-sible way to go was south, through about 100 miles of the vast desert. I thought he was joking. This very desert was known as the "lost-and-found place for weathered goods," meaning that anything that went missing (cats, dogs, pigs, horses, even wives and kids) was 100 percent likely to be found if you went south because no living thing could survive there, and their dead bodies would be kept there forever. Neither of us wanted to be a weathered, lost body at our final ending. However, Lao Jian said that an experienced hunter had shown him a hidden road to pass the desert. We needed to follow a disappeared riverbed, which had dried up a century before, south for three days and then turn east to arrive at a small town called Sazaoshu. Lao Jian said that as long as we followed this route exactly and arrived at that town, we would find the trucks that went there to the oilfields every few days, and we could take such a truck to get to the railway station and make our way home to see our families.

So we began. At midnight, Lao Jian and I crawled out of our cave with water, food, and coats for cold weather that we'd prepared beforehand. We passed a place that had once been full of people but now was utterly silent, and we felt like we were in a cemetery. The moonlight was white, and gullies were crossed everywhere. Those caves were half-buried in the ground; their black semi-circular above-ground openings appeared like hooded eyes. They were literally like tombs for the few persons who were living there, who were almost buried alive.

I recalled my days in those caves, those terrible days of being buried alive like them. Every day some prisoners died. At first it was one or two, later a dozen, then several dozens, just carried out of the caves and abandoned. Living persons, perhaps lying beside you the day before, talking, borrowing water, asking you to help tuck their quilt as they themselves had no strength to do even this themselves, asking you to put a stack of letters, a photo, or embroidered handkerchief into their hands for them to take with. Their temperature, sweat, groaning, the sound of snoring and muttered dream words were still around you, then the next morning they were silent, stiff, shriveled, disappeared, to become bodies nobody could recognize on the yellow sand, left there to become bones.

What is death like? It's nothing special. It's just there. It's around you! It was there at the dusty caves and in the

shadows behind the dim oil lamps. Its face was pale with
hollow cheeks, its hands skinny and shivering like a bird's
claws. Its mouth had smelly breath, and below its eyes there
were dark spots. It was dirty and wretched, but it wasn't vi-
cious. It was a bit shy and pathetic, for it was also in starva-
tion. Mostly we pass by death, but sometimes it takes us, like
when you and your companion escaped the cave one night to
the outside world, and you happened to catch the return car
at dawn while your companion did not. Who can say this was
not a kind of luck? That the place he went was better? There
would be bright sunshine, flowers in full bloom, and abundant food, like in a dream, while you were in a nightmare.
Dreams were like this. People came and then left. They were
alive just now but dead in a moment. But when you opened
your eyes, you always found yourself still at the cave, the
outside covered with grey sky and roaring sand, while inside
there was earth, and only earth.

The road gradually disappeared in the distance and we
suddenly saw a new moon-shaped dune. Lao Jian stopped
at a clump of dry poplar and bent down to have a careful
inspection. He declared that this was the disappeared ancient
riverbed, and we would definitely be out of the desert if we
followed its direction. He added that the roots of these poplar were interweaved, and though these trees were separated
from each other every several miles, even every dozen miles,
or several dozen miles, their roots were connected underground. The hunter also had told him that this was where the
ancient underground watercourse was located. He asked me,
"Can you see that dim, low-lying land? That is the ancient
riverbed." Then we followed it.

We stumbled forward, and since we lay for quite a few
days, we walked weakly and unsteadily, like in a dream, but
our hearts were beating very fast, like a rampaging deer just
released from its cage. The sky was dark but the ground
looked white, and we walked in an unreal realm of silence
and brightness. In this kind of quiet, the barking of one or
two dogs in the distance would make us uneasy. Shortly after

we started out, we heard the sound of a car behind us and were so scared that we immediately rolled into a roadside ditch. Fortunately, the car went in the opposite direction (in fact, nobody would go deep into the desert). At daybreak, everything was strange and silent. The yellow sand seemed endless, and we were already into it.

Lao Jian was Sichuanese. Many years before, the bandit groups he was part of surrendered and joined the government forces. When the troops were demobilized he went to the woodlands and became a forest worker. He was nearly forty-years-old, and all the big actions in his life had been completed, with one exception, and that one sent him to the mine. He explained that he didn't follow "the troop's" arrangement (he regarded those collective actions that he did follow as "the troop's"). During the previous spring, all the workers in the forest were taken to a county theater to see an opera. Stricken with diarrhea, Lao Jian fell behind the others and mistakenly entered through the south gate instead of the west gate. At the south gate there were a lot of people, and trucks stopping there, but they were not there for the opera. In fact, these very trucks were used to bring prisoners to the mine, and among the people gathered some were prisoners, some were guards, and others were the relatives of the prisoners to see them off. Some of them were crying and holding each other, and then chaos ensued.

Lao Jian saw the guards pushing a guy who was embracing his crying wife into the truck, and the man's luggage dropped on the ground during the struggle. Automatically, Lao Jian moved forward and picked up the luggage, just as he himself was grabbed by several hands and put into the truck that was destined to bring him on a no-return-trip.

Afterwards, Lao Jian reran the day's events endlessly through his mind until he traced the matter to its very outset, placing the blame on a suspicious heart. This is how it happened: according to the past habits and the forest's regulations, the Sichuanese Lao Jian always had his supper at the dining room with "the troops," but one evening, a good friend asked him to a farmer's home nearby to enjoy a poached hare, and he agreed. Unfortunately, he ate so much that he couldn't digest it, and consequently suffered from diarrhea. Thus, the next fateful day, he fell behind the others and entered the wrong gate. Therefore, this suspicious hare (Lao Jian even thought that it was merely a rabbit from the nearby farmland), whose hair, appearance, body weight, and even sex were unknown to him, and who disguised itself as steaming delicious food, was actually the secret killer and devil that seduced him into the abyss. If he had eaten his supper at the dining room with the troops, he wouldn't have had the diarrhea; if he hadn't had the diarrhea, he wouldn't have fallen behind; if he hadn't fallen behind, he wouldn't have entered through the wrong gate; and if he hadn't entered through the wrong gate, he wouldn't have met those persons and trucks and would have safely seen the opera and safely returned. So all-in-all, his imprisonment was caused by his not being together with the troops. Every individual should always be with troops, and this could help you resist any attack from either a disguised hare or a beautiful snake. This was the final conclusion that Lao Jian drew from his own unfortunate experience.

It was this same Lao Jian, who advocated always being with the troops, who surprised even himself by taking the opposite tack in planning and implementing this escape, which was completely different from his usual moral standard. Lao Jian's job at the mine was to feed the horses, which afforded him the opportunity to skim a rather large quantity of beans from the horse feed over six months' time. Every night when feeding the horses, he would hold back a handful of black beans from the stable and put them into his coat without being noticed. Many a little makes a mickle over time, and when the famine came he had already stored a great deal, which was hidden in his pillow and accompanied him into dreams every night. I couldn't understand why he did this. Maybe it was from a habit formed in the turmoil era or some kind of premonition of catastrophe? Anyhow, it proved that he did have a vision. With the famine becoming more and more serious, hungry prisoners started to take risks, while the supervision and punishment for stealing also became more and more cruel. More and more prisoners were executed just for stealing a handful of beans or a mouthful of feed for pigs, while Lao Jian stopped taking the risk and became a very law-abiding horse groom. Later, when those horses were killed by the hungry persons and eaten to the last bone, even to its skin, persons dying of hunger became unavoidable, and at that moment those black beans hidden in the pillow by Lao Jian, taking his life's risk, turned out be his (and also my later) secret weapon to defend against death.

I got Lao Jian's help at the last moment, and at that time four prisoners among the six in our cave had died already. The middle-aged one lying beside me just died after he ate a kind of grass that even the horses didn't eat. This kind of grass was scattered in the low-lying salt lands, and there were some sparse grass seeds hanging on the grass shoots which could be collected with much effort. We all knew that the horses didn't eat the grass and its seeds, but we didn't know that the seeds would swell after they got into your stomach, and they would swell several times over, even several dozen times, and stuff your intestines so badly that you were not able to evacuate. I can still remember his appearance when he died: after groaning for three days and nights, his belly looked like a shiny, blue-veined drum, and inside it even the strands of the grassroots could be seen. That night, actually, I also went into a dying state just like the middle-aged guy, but the difference was that he was too stuffed and I was too hungry. When he was groaning with his heavy belly, I felt I was floating like a feather, and I was just one step away from the eternal sleep. But just at this moment, the wheel of fortune launched. It became a visible image and it held my soul, which was flying like a kite. Something warm, round, hard, sticky, and sweaty was put into my mouth, and before my brain could distinguish what it was, my body, my stomach, and my mouth had reacted. They had swallowed it already when I tried to open my eyes. Then came the second one, and when I prepared to swallow it, a rough hand touched my face. In the darkness I saw Lao Jian creeping to me and he said to me, "Chew it slowly and don't make any sound." Next he put them into my hand and now I knew they were beans for horses. Every day sweat's soaking and human body's warming made Lao Jian's pillow a breeding tank. These beans had already gone moldy and germinated, but even so they were not lumps of earth, not broken socks, not those grasses even horses didn't take; instead, they were the beans that would save me from dying. I followed his words and chewed them slowly. Then I felt a stream of heat flow through my whole body.

In the far distance where the dune was dissolved into the air, something like a flame appeared. It was dancing and flying in the sunshine, but when the sun was covered by the clouds, it became a piece of transparent silk cloth moving close to the ground. All the scenes were actually just yellow sand, and they were changing their shapes by the breeze in different lights. But this breeze could change into a whirlwind and engulf horses, persons, and even a house in an instant. I met a whirlwind when I was working. It looked like a wave of smoke when seen from a far distance, rising into the air softly. The upper part of the seemingly weak smoke would sway gently and divide into several segments. Then they would turn into a lotus in full bloom and those petals would become longer and longer until finally they changed into a funnel rising into the sky. Now this funnel was coming, and it was circling above the dune not far from us. Lao Jian held my hand, ran fast to a sheltered soil cliff, and knelt down. We could hear the whistling, which was as if sand, gravel, and rock were struggling with invisible hands before they were sucked into the mouth of the funnel, or like numerous ghosts crying and shouting to fly to the sky for they were eager to enter into the funnel. Lao Jian asked me to cover my ears and close my eyes. We prayed, and our prayers came true! When we opened our eyes, there was only silence around us. Lao Jian and I were already half-buried in the sand. Lao Jian's thick eyebrows were fully covered with a layer of sand, and the sand inside his ears was falling down constantly. We struggled to crawl out and went forward. Can you guess what we saw? On a piece of low-lying land formed after the gravel was all sucked away, a white and clean skeleton was embedded in the seam of rocks.

In the late famine, the death rate increased by several dozen every day. At first, they were buried in a place where a board stood with each name on it for his family's recognition, but later, more and more persons died because of hunger, while fewer and fewer persons could be found to bury them. As a result, those dead bodies were just pulled to the edge of the desert and covered with a layer of sand. For the convenience of those guards' patrol, who were also hungry and listless, the survivors were assembled into several caves, and our cave was one of those for the dying persons. We had been in such a place for such a long time that each of us developed a pair of piercing eyes, which meant that we could distinguish those who might survive from those who were definitely going to die soon even though they looked strong. In fact, all of us could expect our own date of death as well as others'. So long as the guy was still alive, he knew about this more or less. Every day, lying in the cave, our main topic was about who might die earlier and who might die later, and we felt very normal and calm, as if we were discussing about who would get up first the next day or who should have a meal first the day after tomorrow. Those who joined our discussion did die following their own expectations (with a difference of no more than three days, which seemed that death was very punctual and it didn't want to fail your appointment with it and make itself lose face). But Lao Jian and I did survive living on those beans which the others didn't have, and this was the distance between life and death. I knew Lao Jian was shortening his own life for me, for it was obvious that one more day I got the beans, he would have one day less on the earth. However, every time he secretly offered me the beans I couldn't refuse. Instead, I was very much afraid that maybe one night he would not come to me anymore and I would get no more beans to save my life. I was aware of where those beans were hidden, and I could observe his movements in the darkness. My conscience didn't allow me to steal those treasures but it didn't cause me to refrain from sharing in them. Every night I was expecting those beans, a handful of them, ten pieces altogether, no more and no less. Every time he calculated carefully before he passed them to me and I would do it again in the darkness. When I was lying there, pretending to receive them surprisingly and happily, I always silently counted the quantity through sensing them by my fingers or my tongue. I was very careful to compare whether it was more than the day before or less than the day before. If I thought it was less than the day before, I would be very nervous for I worried that perhaps Lao Jian was already short of them and his support to me would come to an end. When I thought it was one or two pieces more than the day before (this case seldom happened, I must say), I also felt upset, for I worried that without strict rationing Lao Jian's store might run out soon. Next, the unavoidable thing happened: fewer beans were given. Now I knew I should refuse Lao Jian's sacrifice for me, and several times I already made up my mind to do so, but when Lao Jian's rough hand touched me and when I was so hungry that I became dizzy and dying, my shameless hand opened.

I survived in this way with my gratitude and shame to Lao Jian. I thought Lao Jian's shame should be less than mine, for at least he saved me. But who knows? It's quite possible that his shame was deeper and greater than mine. Every time he heard those dying persons' groaning and sighing, he just turned around and faced the darkness as if he fell asleep, but I knew that he didn't go to sleep at all. He was also suffering, for he just watched them dying without doing anything, though the beans hidden in his pillow might save them. I could understand him, and I guessed that only because of this shame he decided to save my life at the cost of reducing his remaining life by half. Although he didn't take all the beans out for equal distribution (in that case, his own life would be reduced dramatically). However, I still thought he was a saint, for he absolutely didn't have to give those beans to me, and nobody would know about it and nobody would blame him, while the reality was he did give them to me. Just because of this, he was already a saint. No matter what happened later, and no matter what he did later.

I also considered another person a saint. We didn't expect that the slim and pale-faced doctor would be brought to our cave by two guards. I had met him once at his clinic (though very simple, it should nonetheless be referred to as a clinic) where he was wearing a doctor's white overalls. We were all prisoners, but he was different from us who had to do the hard work. He didn't talk much with others and he always looked worried, but he was very careful when treating the patients and he was polite to us, the miners. Lao Jian said that the doctor was a good man, because once when he had diarrhea and made his trousers dirty, the doctor treated him patiently. He even took a specimen with a cotton swab for examination under a microscope, and he also brought clean clothes for Lao Jian to change into. Lao Jian still felt embarrassed when he mentioned the matter. We didn't expect the doctor to be brought there, because we didn't think a man capable of saving a desperate patient would himself die. So his arrival made us realize the seriousness of the situation. Once he removed his doctor's white overalls and left his equipment and medicines, we saw that his weakened health brought him perhaps closer to death than us. We didn't expect that he could survive very long. We knew that he had an advantage, which was his wife, who was like the ancient lady, Meng Jiangniu. She came from a thousand miles away to bring him food and clothing, but we also knew that with the coming of the famine, every time the woman left, the guards would immediately take his food away. They didn't take the food away when the woman was present—they wanted her to come again and bring more food that they could steal. The poor and weak doctor could enjoy the food only once, when his wife was present, and of course he tried to hide some but that was too little compared with what was confiscated. Last time I heard the doctor advise his wife in a low voice not to come and bring him food, and certainly she didn't take his advice, so they had a quarrel. The doctor didn't want his wife to feel sad, so he didn't tell her the truth, but after she kept asking the reason he must have told her. I couldn't understand their words except one sentence that the doctor told his wife in his low voice with his southern accent, "Anyway, there is no use doing it." Then his wife cried quietly because she was afraid the guards would overhear them and, in that case, what the doctor was eating might be taken away. How did the doctor endure the last several months without the extra support? We didn't know. Lao Jian attributed this to the possibility that the doctor noticed the death in advance. Lao Jian said that they knew each other very well, because it was only a doctor who could be against the death, so the death should give some respect to the doctor.

When the food became less and less until there was only soup provided, and when he became weaker and weaker until he nearly collapsed, the doctor would know better than all of us about death's path and omens, but he was always quiet as if he had been in a remote and permanent meditation with the arrival of the dying moment.

"Little guy, are you still alive?" asked Lao Jian, who was lying in the half-darkness. Every morning we greeted each other this way. This was not a joke, because not everyone could answer it and, in fact, every day several persons couldn't answer it and their silence declared their permanent absence.

"I went to the king of hell, but he didn't accept me," I answered.

"Ha ha—it seems he doesn't like you and me. OK, in this case let's be companions one day more," Lao Jian said happily.

Then we noticed the doctor, who slept in the opposite corner. Lao Jian said, "From yesterday afternoon until now, the southern scholar" (Lao Jian always called the doctor this) "has been motionless there. Perhaps he is only two steps away from death."

"You made a wrong calculation—I'm a little bit more than two steps," the doctor's southern accent sounded from the corner. Another dying day started just like this, and as usual, after each of us confirmed that we were still alive, we began to discuss our respective dreams of the previous night. As usual, all our dreams were about food. I said that I dreamed I went back to my own home, and my mother cooked braised pork for me. Lao Jian's dream was like this: he worked as a cook in a big restaurant, and the kitchen smelled delicious and smoky. He was serving the food—dishes such as Kung Pao Chicken, steamed meatballs, and braised octopus— from the oily pot into plates with a long-handled spoon. He served one plate after another, and there was a long line for the plates. It seemed the food in the pots was so plentiful that he could never empty them. Though he was so hungry that he wanted to eat something himself, there was always some- one waiting beside him and he had no chance to stop.

We asked the doctor what he dreamt. After keeping silent for a while, he said he dreamt he went into a white room with- out doors or windows. I thought this dream was quite weird. It was not horrible, but there was something gloomy about it that I couldn't explain. I asked how this could be, because without a door how could you enter the room? The doctor said that he didn't know, but he was standing in such a room with snow-white walls, empty, with no door and no window. Lao Jian didn't make any comment, but on the second day he told me that what the doctor dreamt was actually his death.

That day, after we discussed our dreams, Lao Jian asked the doctor the reason he was brought there. I immediately pricked up my ears, for this had been what we all wanted to know. The doctor made no answer. In order to avoid embar- rassment, I hurried to say that the doctor must be innocent. "Who wouldn't make some minor mistakes? Definitely those officials attempted to frame you—"

"No, I am guilty," the doctor interrupted me. This was really the first time for me to hear somebody say that.

Then Lao Jian said, "Nobody here admitted he was guilty. You, the southern scholar, must be too serious."

"It must be a medical accident, and you didn't do it on purpose," I guessed.

But the doctor answered seriously, "No, I am guilty."

"We are all guilty. I shouldn't have treated those horses badly, and the little guy, I think he was also brought here for no legitimate reason. Am I right, little guy?" Lao Jian asked me.

I answered, "Of course I am not guilty. Lao Jian, you are also not guilty, and the doctor is not guilty, either."

But the doctor said, "No, I am guilty."

We both waited for him to continue, but he said no more. A heavy atmosphere pervaded our cave. Just imagine, this kind guy was just dying, but he still seriously thought he was guilty. Lao Jian sighed and decided to distribute his treasured beans to us. He said, "This is what is left. Let's live or die together, and even in hell we shouldn't be separated." But the doctor refused. He said that several beans each day were just like a drop in the bucket and could save none of us, so it would be better that Lao Jian and I shared them and maybe we could survive a few more days. We knew his suggestion was correct.

I asked the doctor how he could survive without the beans, and he answered mysteriously, "I have my own way and you will see."

I guessed that he might have some secret weapons, just as Lao Jian had the beans, and this made me feel a little envious. But unexpectedly, the reality was that he would rather die than accept Lao Jian's assistance. He refused Lao Jian's life-saving rope at the last moment. He didn't wake up the next day. He lay quietly in the corner, not able to answer our inquiries anymore. Like all the other persons who starved to death in their dreams, he looked serene.

When you read this you might realize that the night when Lao Jian and I escaped, we had actually run out of everything.

The day before we left we had eaten up all the beans hidden in his pillow. So what could we depend on to sustain the five-day journey through the desert? Do you know what the "food" was when I wrote that we started off with the food and coats for the cold weather?

This was Lao Jian's secret. The night before, he left the cave secretly and brought back something wrapped with paper. He put it into the bag used for beans before and hid the bag under his pillow. He told me that was our food.

The night in the desert was very cold. The temperature difference between day and night might have been forty degrees. In order to seek refuge from the extreme hot and cold moments, we took a rest at the hottest hours in the daytime and hurried on our way in the morning, at sunset, and at night. But we had no idea where we were or whether we could escape the desert. We had already walked three days and nights, but the expected town didn't appear. We must have gotten lost, or, in other words, we went to the wrong direction unconsciously. We had no compass or map, and the scene before us was always the same: the yellow sand all over the place, weathered cliffs seen occasionally, jagged black stones, as well as some sparse red willows and camel thorns.

Neither of us mentioned about getting lost, and we didn't even mention the ancient riverbed that once brought us hope, which was already covered by the boundless sand and concealed from our view. On the first two days, Lao Jian sometimes stopped to decide whether we were already on the riverbed, but soon he didn't do it anymore. After that day's storm, Lao Jian changed. He became silent and absentminded, and I couldn't find out what he was thinking. Maybe the bones reminded him of something or he realized something? But in the desert there were thousands of such corpses! So I didn't understand what stirred up his feelings so much.

That night we rested in a small cave under a soil cliff. When I almost went to sleep in the hazy moonlight, I found

Lao Jian sitting beside me, looking around aimlessly, as if there were an invisible rope pulling his sight here and there. He muttered something. I asked him what he said, but he said he didn't say anything. I told him that I was sleepy, then he said, "You just go to sleep, and have a nice sleep," like coaxing a child. He also patted my head with his rough hand.

I went to sleep immediately. I saw myself walking in the desert but, to be accurate, I was flying or floating in the air one foot above the ground. I just flew and floated without any difficulty and very soon I arrived at the place where the day before Lao Jian and I experienced the whirlwind. Those bare rocks were standing there vividly. Since I was half-floating in the air (I floated higher now), I could easily see the whole terrain below. A riverbed appeared clearly. I was wondering whether this was the very riverbed mentioned by Lao Jian, then suddenly I saw a man walking along the riverbed. From where I was, I could see only the top of his head, like a very small seed, moving slowly in the yellow sand. I couldn't recognize him, but I was sure he was not Lao Jian. As a matter of fact, there were not only we two in this desert. I sighed in relief, and realized that this guy knew the way, while Lao Jian and I got lost. I told myself we should follow him and then we would arrive at that town soon. While saying this to myself, I did see several grey roofs, just like what Lao Jian described, small ones located at the edge of the desert and the end of the riverbed. Their shape was like toy brick and I almost could touch them. I also saw a road winding through these houses, and a truck with oilcans on it stopping there. So this meant the hunter was right! I couldn't help shouting, "We will succeed very soon!" I wanted to fly to the truck (in fact, I already floated there), but suddenly I remembered Lao Jian, who was sleeping under a soil cliff, worried about losing the way. I thought I had to return and wake up Lao Jian. While thinking this, I woke up.

I woke up and saw myself lying in the cave, and Lao Jian was not at my side. I thought he might have gone for a pee or to explore the way, so I rolled over, feeling very sleepy.

Suddenly I became sober and trembled with fear for I saw there was another person at the deep end of the cave! It was a man, his back to me, hunched at his waist, half-lying down, one elbow supporting his body and the other arm moving to wipe away the sand and the pebbles under him in order to lie in a more comfortable and smooth place. For us living in caves for so long, these were quite familiar postures, but this guy was not Lao Jian. I sat up with a start and asked, "Who are you?"

"What did you say?" Lao Jian asked behind me, and I turned back and found Lao Jian was back, looking at me nervously. I looked in that direction again, but didn't see anything under the bare earth wall. I asked Lao Jian where he had been and, with his eyes twinkling a little, he hesitantly said that he went out to catch a breath. Then he asked me exactly what I saw just then. I told him I seemed to see a person. He was startled, and asked, "A person? What kind of person?" I told him there was a man who was just in our cave. His expression solidified and he managed a smile as if to say I was still asleep. I said that was possible, then he didn't say anything more. When I lay down again, I told him that I had dreamt about the ancient riverbed as well as a man who was walking along it. Lao Jian just said, "Oh!" without any other comment. I continued to say that the man knew the way, and he was not me or him. Lao Jian coughed and asked whether we knew the man. I said I didn't see him clearly. Lao Jian kept silent for a while and then told me to go on sleeping. I slept again in a daze, but I didn't sleep well. I was disturbed by something and, uneasy, I felt vaguely that Lao Jian might know something that he concealed from me.

On another night my premonition was confirmed. We didn't find any town or road yet that day, and we were trapped in a great depression. At night we rested under another soil cliff. I felt very tired and low-spirited and went to sleep easily in such a state. When I woke up, Lao Jian had disappeared. The big round moon was half-covered by a mass of black clouds, as if someone dripped an ink-drop into a white porcelain pot filled with clean water, then slowly the ink-drop blurred bigger and bigger. Meanwhile, the big shadow of the clouds cast on the ground was moving on the shining white sand, just as some invisible persons were walking. I closed my eyes and remembered the back of the man that I saw accidentally the night before. Suddenly I had a presentiment, so I held my breath and, as expected, I heard someone speaking: "You needn't say things like this, which makes you like an outsider. We are now a family, tightly bound together. You just rest assured, safe and sound. Even if the sky falls down, I am here. No problem. I know the way, and I am strong. I will definitely take you out of the desert."

I recognized Lao Jian's voice without any difficulty at all, and the voice was from the soil cliff above my head. I was sure that he climbed there when I was asleep, but with whom was he talking? The hairs on my back stood up. I was wondering whether I should go there to see what was happening. At this moment I heard Lao Jian laughing an easy and hearty laughter, which was totally different from his worried look in the daytime. He said, "I should leave now, and you just have a good sleep. The little guy will be frightened if he can't find me."

He walked toward me with rustling footsteps on the gravel, so I hurried to close my eyes. I heard him step slowly and lightly when he approached me and then he sat down. He must have been looking at me, for I could feel his warm breath on my face. I opened my eyes abruptly, which made him a little startled. I asked him whom he spoke.

A shadow swept across his face, perhaps a moon's shadow. He appeared surprised and asked, "What do you mean, 'Whom did I speak to?'"

I told him that I heard what he said just now. With my hand pointing to the cliff above my head, I said that I heard him speaking to someone.

Lao Jian's face brightened, and the moon's shadow moved away. He smiled and told me he was just talking to himself. "You know, I like speaking to myself when I urinate."

I didn't believe him. Although I was scared to death, I still decided to go up to the soil cliff to see what happened. I found the sandy soil there had been trodden into a smooth area, and someplace up there a pool of urine stains could be seen. But the sandy soil was so soft that no complete footprint could be kept. Reluctantly, I went back, but I stopped after taking several steps. How should I judge those footprints? They were too many and too disorderly for only one person. Couldn't there be another person's footprints among them? A shiver ran down my spine. I looked around but didn't see anything except a silent desert, boundless, in the dark blue night sky.

When I went back down, Lao Jian had already closed his eyes and he looked very tired. I suddenly felt very hungry, and I told him so. Still with his eyes closed, he told me that the food was in my coat and asked me to take it by myself. I asked when he had put the food into the pocket of my coat, but he didn't reply. I took out a packet wrapped in a piece of old newspaper whose color was already dark and gloomy, and looking stiff and dirty. I untied it layer by layer, then brought out something half-dried and bloody. I bit off a piece. Although it tasted sticky and bloody, it was very tender. I was so hungry that I bit off another two or three pieces in an instant. I asked Lao Jian whether he wanted to eat some and, with his eyes still closed, he answered that he already ate. I didn't know when he ate, for I never saw him eating. I thought maybe he ate when I was asleep. I found that he looked glum, so I reluctantly wrapped the leftover portion in the newspaper, for I thought I should leave some for him. You must have known that it was a piece of meat. Lao Jian said he had stolen the newly-killed horse meat from those guards. I said I was told long ago that there was no more horse left, and he said this was the last one.

I lay down side by side with Lao Jian. What had happened in the last several days crowded into my mind. I told Lao Jian that since only we two were left, he must trust me. As if he were asleep, he didn't reply. Then I told him that I trusted him, and no matter what happened I would trust him, so he also should trust me. Lao Jian was still motionless, but his eyelashes were moving, so I knew he must have heard my words.

The next day he talked even less. We walked and walked, feeling very exhausted. We were more sleepwalking than actual walking, and we did this for a few days and couldn't stop. Lao Jian was walking beside me, but I had a strange feeling that he was also taking care of someone else by the arm at his side from time to time, and one of his arms stretched out to hold something, which made him look very uncomfortable. One time he stooped for no reason to pull up something, as if there were a person's arm; another time he stopped, looked behind him, and when I found him falling behind, I went back to him only to hear him muttering some words in the direction behind him, like, "Let me carry you." I asked him who he was talking to, but he didn't answer. Instead, wiping his forehead, he said that we had a long way to go.

Approaching noon, we took a rest in a small valley. I unbuttoned my coat and took out a pile of letters, which were the doctor's. According to the regulations, these relics should be taken away by the guards, but somehow they were left in our cave. These letters were written to him by his wife. Every time she came, besides the life-saving food, she would also bring these letters. After she left, the doctor would carefully hide those biscuits (sometimes he would share some with us) and lay down (this was the best posture to save our body strength) to read those letters again and again. We didn't know what was written in them, so we really felt envious. Every time his wife got down into our cave and sat beside her husband in a corner, with the dust of a long, arduous journey and a fresh scent of female from the outside world, we were sensitive enough to turn round. They jabbered in a southern accent unknown to us. It was just like a kind of bird language to me, but it warmed my heart and made me want to cry.

Nobody knew how the weak and shy woman saved these foods in such a famine era and trekked a few thousand miles from the south to come there, but I knew the doctor became restless several days before she came. Again and again he wiped and tidied up his suit, which was almost worn out, but he always wore it when his wife came. And he tried by all means to get a washbasin of water, which, you know, was so precious in the Gobi Desert, so sometimes he could only get some swill for pigs. With a kind of method that none of us knew (it was said that all the doctors knew it), he got rid of the smell and used such a kind of water to wash his face and wipe his body carefully. Then his wife came. When we still had the strength to leave the cave, they could spend a few hours in the cave alone. At their last meeting, he could only sit on his bunk to greet her, for he couldn't stand up anymore. He told his wife that he accidentally sprained his foot at work, and he didn't tell her that the last time, as soon as she had left, the guards burst into our cave and took away all the food she brought him.

Quite often, I remembered the couple during our journey, which was not only because he was the last one to leave us at the cave, but also because we took his letters with us. The thick wad of letters was hidden in the pocket of his coat. I found them when I took his coat. Lao Jian disapproved of my taking the coat, and even became angry when he saw me carrying these letters. But I told him that in case we could actually escape, and in case we had the chance, perhaps we would give back these letters to his wife, and he didn't object anymore.

Another reason for me to carry these letters, which I didn't tell you yet, was that I wanted to know what crime the doctor had committed. I had already read many of them, but couldn't find any clue yet. This noon I brought them out again from my coat. I opened one, written in a student's exercise book (so I guessed his wife might be a teacher), and the handwriting was small, delicate, and clear. When I was holding it, I seemed to see her just in front of me. After I gave a cough, I told Lao Jian I would read him something, and before he could say anything, I started.

"Dear Wen, I have been thinking about your words about being guilty. I kept thinking but I can't understand your meaning. You are undoubtedly a good person, an innocent person, so why do you think that you are guilty? OK. Let's not discuss the matter, otherwise we will quarrel again. Our parents are well and in good health, and I am sure they can't wait to see you back. But I worry about you most. Well, I'd like to tell you some good news: Maomao was teething with his first tooth yesterday. When I was feeding him milk, I found him biting the rubber nipple, not loosening. I pulled it but couldn't, so I thought maybe he was teething. I put my finger into his mouth, and he bit it at once. I could feel my finger being pricked by two pointed things up and down, and it hurt! So I shouted, 'Maomao, stop! You are hurting Mom!' And it seemed he understood my words, but he didn't open his mouth and still ground with all his exertion—"

"Stop!" Lao Jian suddenly sat up and shouted. He grabbed the letter from my hand and said, "Why don't you let him take a rest? He walked with us for one day and he is tired! We still—" At that moment, he remembered something and stopped.

I asked, "Lao Jian, what are you talking about? Who walked with us?"

Lao Jian answered impatiently, "It's him! Can't you see him? Can't you see him?"

He puffed and panted, his mouth half-open, expressionless, as if too much blood had gushed to his face and caused a blockage. I held his hand and stroked his back. He didn't throw me off, perhaps because he had no strength to do so. After a while, he calmed down and asked me what he had said just then.

I didn't have the heart to look at him, so I just said that he was too tired.

He bowed his head, and murmured, "Yes, I am too tired."

Now the situation became clear, and I knew that the third person was with us. In fact, I had had this sense long before. In the desert, boundless desert, especially in those desolate

nights when Lao Jian and I walked unsteadily, I could feel
another person following us—no, not following us but, to
be exact, walking on the other side of Lao Jiao. Three of
us walked side by side together. But because Lao Jian was
between me and him, I couldn't see him clearly. He walked
silently. When we stopped, he also stopped; when we started,
he also started; and when we rested, he also rested, just as a
very quiet and coordinated member among us. Many times
I heard his breath, his heavy footsteps, and his panting. And
when I walked before Lao Jian, I still could feel another
moving shadow behind Lao Jian's stout shadow. Sometimes
in my sleep when I was only half-asleep, I could clearly see
his back. (It seemed he always showed me his back.) He was
either lying on the other side of Lao Jian or sitting there,
busy with something. He murmured something. But when I
opened my eyes and approached him to see more clearly, he
disappeared. Even so, now I was certain without any doubt
that he did exist, which was not only because I could feel
this, but also because Lao Jian could see him and he was
even determined to take him with us. I believed this became
the only reason for Lao Jian to try to survive. Lao Jian supported him (I mentioned this action before), held him (this
was another action I quite often saw), and sometimes I could
see Lao Jian carrying him on his back. Lao Jian bent down
with his two hands backward, holding up something on his
hip. Because of the invisible weight, Lao Jian's breath became heavy and short, and his face became distorted. Many
times I could see clearly that his footprints on the sand were
deeper down, so his burden was obvious and worrying. But
Lao Jian never allowed me to help him. Every time when
I asked to help him to carry "that person" on my back, he
refused very angrily. He even denied that there was such a
person in order to refuse me completely. His attitude made
me believe that there was a secret between him and "the person," but what the secret was, I didn't know.

That night when I woke up, Lao Jian wasn't there as before, but his coat was spread on the ground and our food,

that piece of meat, which was shrunken and dried and whose color had turned dark red, was placed at the breast place of his coat, which at first glance looked like a piece of meat or an organ from a human body. This discovery suddenly made my heart tighten, and some terrible associations stiffened my arms and legs and I couldn't move at all. I asked myself why I didn't discover this earlier? I tried to get up and I stood, leaning on the soil cliff, and walked to the back of the soil cliff. Unexpectedly, I saw a river! A real river, just lying on the sand, shining under the moonlight as if it were a big fish! The light of the big fish hurt my eyes. I covered my eyes, then I faintly saw Lao Jian sitting at the riverside, his back toward me, and beside him there was another person. Immediately I knew he was that person, the third person who was always with us, and now I could see him. I saw Lao Jian kneeling on the ground and washing him. When I went closer, I found the guy was the doctor. Lao Jian was washing the doctor's leg wound. "You don't have to feel sad about this. I don't feel pain at all." This was the doctor's voice, still with the southern accent as before, which was quite clear at night. "You forget, now we will not feel pain anymore." In order to prove his words, the doctor smiled, exposing his snow-white teeth, and his smile looked young and bright in the moonlight.

Lao Jian murmured, "No, please let me wash it for you, then I can feel better," and he worked harder to use the cotton to clean the doctor's bloody leg, to be exact, to block the outflow of blood from the wound. But his efforts were useless, for the balls of cotton thrown from his hands all turned red like flowers, but the blood was still gurgling out, just like numerous red streams which even turned the river red.

I was totally stunned. I wasn't surprised at the doctor being there at this moment, and actually in my consciousness I had already vaguely felt that the "third person" was the doctor. Instead, what surprised me was the doctor's leg wound. It was not indeed a wound, but a very large surface of a wound. In other words, a large piece of muscle of one of his inner thighs was carved out, and it was carved so completely that even his bone could be seen. I didn't remember when the doctor got such a wound in his leg, because in my memory he was intact when he was carried out of the cave. I remembered clearly the day when he was moved out—his face was pale and calm, arms and legs intact, no bloodstain on his body, just like in a deep asleep. So what the hell happened?

What happened? I thought and asked—maybe blurted out. Actually, there was no need for me to ask the question, for both of them knew what I wanted to know. They turned around, looking at me. Lao Jian's eyes were blood-red and he grabbed my arm.

I woke up, finding myself lying under the soil cliff. Lao Jian was facing me, holding my arm with one of his hands. There was no doctor at his side, but his eyes were still as blood-red as in my dream. I remembered my dream, and realized that I didn't truly wake up until now. But who could know this was not another dream? I looked at Lao Jian nervously, for I sensed that he wanted to tell me something. I waited, and our eyes met, but his eyes shrank back like a snail's tentacles, and blood also retreated from his face and eyeballs, leaving his face grey and his appearance haggard, just like a wood carving. I wanted to talk about the dream just now, the doctor as well as the bloody leg, but I didn't know why I couldn't open my mouth. Some kind of premonition held me back. I was like a person already walking to the edge of an abyss, who clearly knew that he was at the brink but refused to look at the dark chasm just under his feet. I opened my mouth, but said something totally different. I said that we would never get out of there.

Lao Jian forced a smile and stroked my face with his hand. He reassured me and said that I still could survive several days with the remaining food. Hearing the word "food," my heart tightened. I asked him why he said it like that, for the food was also his. Lao Jian froze momentarily, then agreed in a hoarse voice.

From my dream I remembered the shape of the meat in Lao Jian's pocket, and my heart clenched so tight that I couldn't even breathe. I abruptly wanted to do something, so I brought out the food from my coat. It had become darker and drier, but was not rotten yet. It was lighter than the day before because of the loss of moisture. I bit off a piece, and inexplicable fear and nausea blocked my throat. I did retch a bit and the bloody meat dropped on the ground. Tears welled up in my eyes, and I looked at Lao Jian. I told him I couldn't eat. I really couldn't eat.

Lao Jian collapsed like a piece of wood, sitting on the white sand. He opened his mouth to try to say something, but he couldn't. I heard a strange voice sounding from his dry mouth. He frowned, laughing or perhaps crying. Something wet appeared in the corners of his eyes filled with sand but dried immediately, like salt.

"Eat. If you can eat you will have hope, otherwise how can you leave here?" he said, laughing and crying.

I kept vomiting, my empty stomach convulsing painfully, which meant it refused the meat although it could save my life. I threw it on the ground.

Lao Jian crawled there, dug a grave with his hands, put the meat into it, and then covered it with a handful of sand. We two dying persons erected a tomb for our last food. Our hearts gradually calmed down, and we looked at it slowly turning aglow by the sunset.

He murmured to ask me to listen. I wiped away my tears and tried to listen attentively. I couldn't hear anything, but there was indeed some faraway sound. A woman was crying, constantly crying, because a piece of meat was scooped from her husband's leg. What a sin it was!

Lao Jian muttered, "But now she wouldn't cry anymore."

I told him that I didn't blame him and I knew no matter what he had done, it was to save me.

Lao Jian smiled weakly and told me that he had thought like this before.

I gasped that I must tell him something, really—otherwise, I was afraid there might not be any chance. I told him that I said I was innocent before and I was a scapegoat for others, but actually —

Lao Jian interrupted me, "I understand."

I asked, "Lao Jian, can you forgive me?"

Lao Jian touched my hair with his hand and said, "Little guy, the doctor said we were all guilty, so how can I not forgive you?"

He didn't say more, and for a good while I thought he was asleep. I asked whether we were still in a dream.

Lao Jian answered with difficulty, "No, it's not a dream. He's here with us. No matter what happens, you shouldn't forget him, or leave him. You must take him out..."

And he toppled down slowly, just like a broken tree.

The rest of the time, I walked alone in the desert. I was determined to survive not only because of Lao Jian's request, but also because of my belief that the doctor was also walking with me. So I knew that I must bring him out of the desert. And as long as I could leave there, I could give him and those letters back to his wife, the great woman, as well as that meat, which I restored to the doctor's leg in my dream.

One day before I was going to leave the desert, there was a strong wind. At night, I followed what Lao Jian had taught me, to hide behind a soil cliff. The wind had been blowing for three days and nights, and I just hid in the cave piled by gravel. It was very quiet, like Noah's Ark. There was a soft light in the cave and I didn't know where it was from, but the light made me feel serene and I could even read by the light. I took out the doctor's letters, which I didn't read anymore after Lao Jian died. I read,

When you are reading the letter, I am in the returning truck, farther and farther away from you, and you must be lying in that dark cave, that very dark and dusty cave. You have been there for a whole year, which made me feel very sad every time when I thought of this. How can you survive? What can you do without food? But after a while I felt a little better. Do you know the reason? I thought of your companions suffering with you, who are also miserable. I realized that guilty persons would not be lonely. The main reason was from a story I read, which you know, about what Jesus told his disciples. Jesus said, "What do you think? If a man owns a hundred sheep, and one of them wanders away, will he not leave the ninety-nine on the hills and go to look for the one that wandered off?" Jesus then said, "If he finds it, I tell you the truth, he is happier about the one sheep than about the ninety-nine that didn't wander off."

I listened to the outside and found that the wind had stopped. I tried to get out but found all exits were blocked by sand. I didn't feel worried, however. Instead, I was very calm. I didn't have to worry about how to make my way out from the cave almost buried by the sand, for I saw that at its entrance, a strong hand was stretching into it, and I was quite sure it was to save me, and I also knew this hand was from him, the doctor, who had been walking with us in the desert. I took the hand.

—February 22, 2004, the second manuscript
—May 13, 2004, the third manuscript

My Left Hand

My right hand doesn't know what my left hand is doing.
                                                    —F. Kafka

You can't understand why Dongzi hoarded up so much toilet paper before he died. Rolls of it were crammed into the ward's closet, erectly and silently, just like soldiers with heavy uniforms. There were hundreds of them. During his three years at the mental hospital, at the visiting hours each Sunday, he asked his family to bring him the toilet paper. Since it was a daily necessity, neither the hospital nor his family could refuse his request, though they felt vaguely that his toilet paper was used too fast and too much. Later on one day, when the hoarded toilet paper was too much to be crammed into the closet, the bedside cabinet, the drawers, as well as under his bed anymore, and there was no other space to store more of it in such a small ward under the monitoring of the nurses, Dongzi hanged himself with a rope from the heating pipe above the window.

You went to the crematorium in the western outskirts the day his body was cremated. Standing in the chilly wind outside the gate of the funeral chamber, you found many persons unknown to you. Their clothing was proper and right, and so was their sadness. Those funeral scrolls on the wreaths outside the gate had been removed, to be replaced by new ones; the several remaining scrolls were blown by the wind, the words on them becoming indistinct. The name of a unit appeared on one of them, which made you remember that Dongzi had been a staff member of a unit, just as you were.

All the persons present expressed their grief restrainedly and decently except Dongzi's silver-haired mother. The funeral music played for each deceased made the whole process seem programmed. After bowing to the remains one after another in a queue, these persons came back to early spring's chilly air and breathed a sigh of relief honestly, and they put the rented white paper flowers into the box at the gate, together with their grief. You arrived just at this moment, and went into the funeral hall following several unknown persons to where the sad funeral music filled the air. When you looked at the huge floral arrangements woven with holly, lilies, and chrysanthemums at the center of the hall, you found that the face of the bloated body lying there was actually strange and unrecognizable to you.

At that moment you shouted silently at your heart in surprise, and your steps became hesitant. But you couldn't be hesitant for too long, for the condolence team was moving forward following the designated route, and you couldn't retreat either, just like a river that already flowed into the sea couldn't flow back to the watercourse. The two persons standing before you had left after a bow, while another two behind you were waiting for your movement. So with hesitation you walked forward or, in other words, forced by others, you had to move forward. You bowed three times to the unrecognized body. At the intervals between the bows, you could see the face in the flowers and you would feel his eyes suddenly becoming alive, revealing a little gap through which the stranger lying amidst the bouquets had already seen your embarrassment, and his calm and pale face gave a sarcastic smile.

Then you shook hands with his relatives like all the other persons. The names on the wreaths and those strange faces further confirmed your doubt, but nobody was surprised at your arrival, and his relatives also expressed the same gratitude to you. A middle-aged dropsy man held your hand tightly and said "thank you" in a low voice, while his elderly mother even grabbed your arm and leaned her head on your chest, and her sobbing words made all the others present convinced of friendly feelings between you and the deceased. At this moment, tears welled up in your eyes, together with sudden grief and sadness, though they both came from nowhere but they were truly sincere because the mother, who you had never known or seen, said, "Until his death my son had been looking forward to seeing you."

You took this as a revelation and a message. Later you knew the truth, that actually you arrived two minutes later, after Dongzi's photo and body had been moved out of this funeral hall. But these words, like a secret code, connected you and Dongzi together although you and he were in two different worlds. This was what Dongzi left you, because a few days before, at his dusty home, his mother had said the same thing. She said, "My son had been looking forward to seeing you until his death."

Now when you are typing these words on the keyboard, your vision is at the northern Shannxi Plateau thousands of miles away, through those high buildings and grey streets. The factory, a small local factory making cement where you and Dongzi once worked, was located there. Everything there looked yellow—yellow rivers, yellow land. Piles of loess hills stretched for thousands of miles and looked like squeezed semi-solid, semi-liquid toothpaste, and at the foot of them the Yan River, which had been sung about countless times, meandered through. This was a typical northern river, sometimes quiet and clean and sometimes roaring and muddy. You seemed to have sighted two young men barefoot at the river, fishing. They were you and Dongzi. You wore faded grass-green uniforms, and since the trousers were rolled up, your suntanned and strong lower legs were exposed. Dongzi's back was to you, so you could see clearly his thick, weed-like hair. How much you liked to see him hanging the fish bait and then throwing the long line at the water! It was just like a thin ray of light, gashing the blue air open and finally stopping at the surface of the water vertically, as if it were a secret road to heaven. The terminal point of the road was just at Dongzi's hand, which was firm and steady. His motionless silhouette reminded you of God, yes, God— a hunter with calm assurance. God was holding the fishing rod with his left hand. You will never forget that Dongzi and you were a good pair and no matter what you played, either badminton or table tennis, you played right-handed while he played left-handed.

This was Dongzi's hand, his left hand. The five fingers were short and thick with a small palm, but his wrist was wide. Every bone on his hand was solid and tough, just like the paws of beasts. And his appearance of gripping the racket also made you think of a beast, an alert beast ready to jump out at any moment. Furthermore, it was a born feline killer, such as a tiger whose downy fur bore yellow and black stripes, or a leopard who could shrink into itself in one moment and then become a straight line in another moment. You and he were just two young leopards, jumping side by side all night long. To this very moment you can still smell those nights—yes, not see but smell—when you played table tennis at the cement table in that empty factory building. The sweat from his body smelled salty and wafted to you warmly and constantly, but maybe the smell was from your body and it wafted to him. Your smells had already mixed together to become indistinguishable. Besides, your arms often collided with his, and your feet often tramped on his. You still remember that one time when he accidentally stepped on your foot, you exploded with great anger. On the big toe there was a chunk of bruising that slowly receded and disappeared as time went on.

Now you see Dongzi hugging that dog whose name was Baba. Without Baba, you and he would never have had the chance to get to know each other. On the truck to send the first group of young workers to the factory, Dongzi sat beside you and, like all the other persons, you took him as a local rural guy because he wore dirty, homespun clothes, his lips and face were full of sunburns, and his hands held a pouch made of coarse cloth. When you squeezed yourself in next to him, he said, "Be careful! Don't rest yourself on Baba." You couldn't understand his words, so you asked what he meant. This time he spoke in a loud voice: "Be careful! Don't rest yourself on Baba." His accent was an authentic Beijing accent, but what he said made everybody on the truck laugh. You became upset and warned him to be careful. Dongzi hurried to explain that the Baba he mentioned was a dog, and at the same time he opened the pouch and a furry black head popped out, with its two ears pricking up and barking two times. The whole truck burst into an uproar: "Wow! Your father turned out to be a dog!" Dongzi explained innocently, "This dog's name is Baba." Then all the persons laughed aloud even more.

Later, quite often you could see Dongzi walking the dog. The dog had a black head but its paws were white, and one of its legs was lame so it couldn't walk fast. Several other educated youths also had their dogs. Every day when these dogs met, they would inevitably fight and Baba was always the object to be bullied and ridiculed. Usually the big wolfhound bullied him, while the small pug chased him. Since Baba could neither beat them nor run faster than they ran, he could only follow close behind Dongzi with his tail between his legs. Dongzi and his dog together became a laughingstock for everyone. They said that he not only had a lame dog, but he also called it his father, and they even humiliated him, "If you really need a father, I can be yours—you don't have to find a dog as your father!" They tempted the dog with a bone by forcing it to stand up to get it. They said, "You are such a stupid dog. Look how ugly you are! And you can't even stand up, but you want to be a father?" Then they threw the bone hard at its face. Baba fell backwards while trying to stand up, and looked at the bone, tears in his eyes, but refrained from eating it and walked lamely back to Dongzi. Dongzi kicked him with a glum face, and scolded, "Go eat the bone—just go! You're a bitch!" Baba could understand Dongzi's words and lowered his head ashamedly, lying on the ground, with his legs knelt down.

You were the only person who didn't laugh at Dongzi and Baba. You stroked the poor dog and asked how it became lame. Dongzi told you that when he was asleep at his foot, he accidentally trod on its waist and it was broken. Nobody

expected Baba to survive that winter, but he did survive!
Then Dongzi became proud, and said that though the dog
was not very healthy, it would have a long life. He asked Baba
for a reaction, and the dog seemed to understand his words,
looked up, and gave some sound of agreement. Its eyes were
black and bright, with much beauty and warmth. You asked
why it was given such a strange name, and Dongzi answered
that he had no other choice, for it already had the name when
his neighbor gave it to him. You often saved some mantou for
the dog, and became acquainted with both Dongzi and the
dog. Then one snowy day, Baba fell seriously ill with a high
fever, and you accompanied Dongzi to take the dog to see
the vet who was fifteen li away. But on the way, Baba died
in Dongzi's arms at dawn. You two buried his stiffened body
under a big tree beside the cement factory. Dongzi wrapped
him with his own pillow covers, and you found a box and a
shovel. Looking at the small tomb, Dongzi couldn't help crying although he tried to restrain himself, and the tears flowed
down. Wiping his tears, he felt ashamed for he thought this
was wrong behavior and he begged me not to tell the others that he cried for Baba. You didn't say anything. You just
walked to him and embraced his shoulders. At that moment,
Dongzi cried heartily on your shoulder.

Later Dongzi moved into your dormitory. And at that time,
some grass grew on Baba's small tomb.

Shuizhen

Most workers at the small cement factory located on the banks of the Yan River came from the mountain ravine nearby, and the raw material used for making cement was also from there. Stones were put into large baskets, which were then carried on the backs of very thin donkeys. These donkeys hobbled in a long line on the high slopes along the Yan River, trembling and shaking, with their pointy ears pricking up. They followed the winding path to climb a steep mountain road, then waded through shallow floodlands. They came out of the loess and went into the iron gate of the cement factory. One day every week, as these donkeys entered into the door in a lurch, there would be a lively gathering. It was a gathering both for the donkeys and for those young men and women. When the ore was removed, those sweaty and exhausted donkeys felt relief, so they were braying happily, followed by many people shouting. The young male donkeys became restless when they suddenly found so many female donkeys around them, and this kind of feeling was the same for those sweaty young men. Of course, donkeys behaved more directly. Instead of using eyes or words to flirt with each other, which were unnecessary for them, they just did what they wanted, because usually they were confined in different houses and burdened by heavy millstones, so immediate opportunities were too precious to be wasted. Watching these donkeys free of heavy burdens, breeding eagerly, men would shout excitedly and remind young girls to look at the male donkeys' actions. They might ask the girls to see what the little donkey was doing, and where it leaned. They also might say some nasty words, like, "The little thing is not big, but its penis is so long. Look, something is flowing out. Oh! So much!" And then those girls' faces turned red and they hurried to lower their heads, while those men burst into laughter.

You were just twenty-years-old at that time. The thick dust mask covered your face, while Dongzi's face was also covered by such a mask. Neither of you said anything, but you knew that Dongzi's heart was beating fast, and so was yours. One night you were already in a drowsy sleep, but then you were prodded awake. It was Dongzi. He said that he couldn't go to sleep and asked to get under the quilt.

Among the young workers in the cement factory, every two of them shared one dormitory, which actually was just like a cave located on the hillside inside the factory. At first, the roommates in each room were arranged by the factory, but workers later made adjustments by themselves and formed stable and free combinations. Your original roommate was a young man suffering from insomnia who couldn't stand almost every midnight when Dongzi came to your room noisily to ask you to play table tennis. The roommate volunteered to exchange rooms with Dongzi, and you found out later that Dongzi did that on purpose. When he moved to your room, you found that he was actually very quiet.

You and Dongzi grew up in the same city and went to the northwest countryside at the same time, but you didn't know him until both of you were employed by the cement factory. You believe that if both of you had stayed in the city all the time, you wouldn't have been able to become friends because Dongzi belonged to the kind of kids from *hutong*, while you were from an educated family. At that time, your family had two nannies, one for you and the other for your brother. Your family also had an old-fashioned record player as well as many records, including Beethoven's Ninth Symphony, Beethoven's Sixth Symphony, Chai Kefu Chomsky's works, and Brahms's works. When you listened to this world-famous music while the nanny was washing your feet, Dongzi was playing marbles or patting-paper-folded-triangle in the *hutong*, sniffling and full of mud and dust. However, when you two met at the factory, you became the best of friends and partners. You lived together, ate together, and played together, which was a surprise to many others. In fact, it was a surprise to you, too.

That night when Dongzi moved under your quilt, both of you were motionless for quite a long time. His skin was very dark but very smooth, which was unexpected. When he moved in, that piece of skin on your elbow touched his leg first, then his arm, and sensed his softness. And when his arm touched your body, he dodged as his first reaction, but then just stayed there with no more movement as if nothing happened. You two just lay there rigidly, with the only contact at your arm, like two armies with ulterior motives who kept just a small area reserved for tentative fighting.

You pretended to yawn to cover your embarrassment, for you had never slept with another person under the same quilt, even with your own brother, and so now you felt very uneasy. In order to persuade yourself, you had to imagine Dongzi as your own brother five years younger than yourself. You indeed had a brother who was five years younger than yourself, and who you once took to swim at the park. You still could remember how he tottered into the swimming pool just like a little duck, with a big swim ring at his waist, but you obviously couldn't take Dongzi as your little brother.

Then Dongzi broke the silence and said, "Your quilt is very cold." You didn't answer him. He spoke again and said that the quilt was too cold to have been slept in by a dead person. You made no comment, yet. He said that your cold quilt was just like a grave. You decided to pretend to be asleep.

Then Dongzi touched your leg and said that you were both cold and stiff, like a dead body. You still closed your eyes and said that his feet were stinking, like shit. He laughed and was happy that you finally talked to him. He asked you whether you saw those donkeys in the daytime, and he mentioned that donkeys' penises were so big. You kept silent again, for you were not accustomed to talking about the matter, especially under the quilt.

Dongzi touched you with his hand, and asked again whether you saw it. You sat up suddenly, leaning against the wall. Dongzi asked what was wrong with you.

You said, "Mosquitoes. I feel mosquitoes flying here and there." You jumped to the ground barefoot to look for mosquito-repellent incense, but in the darkness you could feel that Dognzi was watching you.

You tried striking a match, but couldn't succeed. Then Dongzi said he would do it, so he squatted beside you to strike the match. Your hair touched his, and you smelled a heavy odor from his body.

Since you couldn't find a stand to hold the mosquito-repellent incense, Dongzi pierced the point of a pair of scissors into the centre of the incense, and when he did this, your heart tightened a little for no reason.

That night, you told Dongzi about the girl called Shuizhen.

In the first winter when you went to that cement factory, the factory director asked you to join the "supporting for agriculture" working group and to go to the Sujiagou village to "guide" the work there. There were only two persons in the so-called working group: the group leader was your workshop director and you were the only member. This was an enviable job, because it diverted persons' attention to a certain extent—people in the factory would think you went to the village, while people in the village would think you should be in the factory, and then you could enjoy some freedom by taking advantage of their ignorance. You didn't know how you could get such an enviable task. Maybe it was because your silent character made the workshop director feel at ease, or because you had great popularity among the youth. You took your favorite book with you—a complete set of Tang poetry—and when the workshop director was passionate to convene a meeting of the villagers to plan to replace the first secretary by the deputy, or to replace the regular team leader with the vice one, you were just wandering idly in the village, and facing the loess plateau, chanting the phoenix trees and plantain in the ancient people's eyes of hundreds of years before. In the sunny days, you would use your motorized faders brought from your home to barber for the kids in the village. Those kids, mainly boys, either tall or short, filed to you in a long, zigzag line. You carelessly surrounded their dirty necks with an old towel, and pressed and held their heads, round or flat, regular or irregular. Then several dozen eyes would stare at you quietly, and they offered their worship to you heartily when you turned different kinds of head shapes into the same style. This kind of worship was so strong that no matter where you went, you would by followed by a group of such kids who were your faithful guards, and they would yell with running noses to clear the way for you, "Working group is coming! Working group is coming!" They didn't know your name, so they just called you "working group." Just by a toy like motorized faders you got the same prestige as the workshop director got by his unremitting efforts of having endless meetings and struggles. In these villagers' eyes, compared to the workshop director's stern voice and countenance, maybe your motorized faders would embody more authority of the working group, which made you feel very intoxicated with a sense of accomplishment. And you felt you entered into an empire created by yourself instead of a village when you looked at those shiny little heads, shaking in the sun, all over the mountains and plains.

Not only did those kids worship you, but also their parents, and they said, "This young man is very competent, for he can not only read the newspaper, but is also barber. The machine at his hand is much faster than the knife of the barber, and he is quite skilled at using it."

The workshop director was very satisfied with your performance, not only because you could barber, but also because you were totally indifferent to those meetings and decisions. Your indifference was so complete that one night when you were awakened by an inexplicable noise and found there was one more pair of women's shoes under the *kang* of the workshop director, who shared the same room with you, and that his quilt was obviously bulging, you kept deaf and blind. The second day, you asked to move elsewhere with an ingenious reason, and he immediately agreed. The master of the house where you moved to stay had a little boy, and a girl who was very pretty—which you didn't realize at that time—and her name was Shuizhen.

People often commented that women in the northern Shannxi were beautiful, while the women in Sujiagou were more beautiful, and Shuizhen's beauty was eye-catching even in Sujiagou. She had a fair complexion, and her white skin was as delicate as the luster of jade. Many years later when you saw a jade goddess of mercy at a relics exhibition, its refinement, slimness, and texture all made you remember Shuizhen. But that winter, Shuizhen was just a village girl with braided hair, not tall, wearing a thick, cotton-padded jacket made of printed cloth with white plum flowers blossoming on a rough, dark blue base. When you entered the house, following the workshop director and carrying your luggage, Shuizhen was wiping the cover of a box—the only furniture in the cave, which could be used both as a box and as a table—positioned beside the *kang*. She stole a glance at you with the corner of her eyes, her lashes hanging low, and left the room with a twist of her body. The workshop director stared at her back for quite a long time, and after coughing a little for no reason, he said, "Hey, young boy, you are coming to a good place."

That night, when you were reading on the *kang*, covered by your quilt, there was a knock on the door and a girl entered with a handful of corn stalks. Lowering her head and not looking at you, she said that her father asked her to add something to your *kang*. You thanked her and told her to put down the firewood for you to do by yourself. She agreed and put it down, but she didn't leave. Instead, she turned around and closed the door, squatted down, and put the firewood into the hole of the *kang* piece by piece. You felt embarrassed and didn't know what you should do. You were so young at that time that you couldn't understand what it meant when a girl went alone to a single man's room at midnight to add firewood for him in the countryside. You could only sense that she was doing this very slowly, and her face, looking at the hole of the *kang*, was too red. Besides, you found that at such a late night, her hair was combed neatly and she had even tied her plait with a piece of red yarn, which was hanging at her breast. And she was wearing a brand-new red cotton-padded jacket printed with the Chinese word for happiness, which should be worn only during Chinese New Year.

You pretended to be reading but couldn't, so you just stared at those black words on the white paper in vain and you felt blank. The north wind outside the window was blowing, the fire was burning more and more briskly, and her face was becoming redder and redder. Your face was also becoming red little by little, which meant that what the firewood was heating was not only the *kang* under your body. But you couldn't move because you had taken off your trousers. Did the girl understand your embarrassment? Or did she find out your secret? She didn't raise her head but her long lashes were quivering. Occasionally you caught a glance from her, which was sweeping over your quilt. She wore a small sly and thoughtful smile. Then she stood up, took a deep breath, and said that it was alright now and you could have a warm sleep. She raised her eyebrows when she spoke and she gave you a quick glance.

Your heart was softly touched by the expression in her eyes. There was something watery in her expressions, floating to you glitteringly. Your face became redder without cause, and your heart beat faster. You said, "Thank you."

She didn't speak, perhaps because she wasn't accustomed to your politeness, and she felt the distance between you and her. She looked a little disappointed but didn't want to give up. So she played with the end of her plait, and looked at the cover of the box with books on it as if thinking about those books or thinking about something else or waiting for something, sometimes stealing a glance toward you. Suddenly she said, "I will bring you a bottle of water." Without waiting for your reply, she hurried to take the thermos from atop the box and went out of the door quickly, as if you might stop her.

You hurried to put on your trousers for you knew she would come back again to deliver the water. You really couldn't understand why she did this, but you could sense that the girl felt love for you, wanted to attract your attention, and was expecting something. However, you didn't know what the hell she wanted or, to be exact, instead of not understanding, you actually understood but you just didn't want to admit it to yourself. You had heard before that the girls in this area liked male-educated youth, and they were particularly fascinated with those young men from Beijing, but you didn't expect that you yourself would qualify. Nevertheless, you clearly knew that nothing would happen, at least from your side. Recognizing the truth of this, you felt very sad when you thought of the beautiful girl.

The door opened and she appeared, carrying the thermos bottle. She stopped with surprise when she saw you standing there, well dressed. You didn't ask her to come in. You took the water from her hand, thanked her, and told her you would do it by yourself. With these words, you put the thermos bottle on the box. The girl stood at the door looking at you, with her black eyes open wide, full of expectation. But you put your hand on the door handle and looked at her condescendingly, for you were much higher than she. Without the slightest hesitation, your body blocked the way by which she might come inside and you asked slowly, "Do you have anything else? It's very late."

The girl's eyes looked at you steadily, as if something in your sound hypnotized her, or as if something in your sound, just like an eraser, wiped her original colorful mind into a blank. She listened word by word, and then tried to understand you word by word. She needed to time to digest your complete meaning after all the words were combined into one sentence. In the end she understood, and the smile on her face became frozen as some invisible water hidden behind her thin skin froze slowly. Her face suddenly turned white and, with a twist of her body, she left you.

The door of the landlord at the yard gave a creak, and inside it the landlord gave a cough, then there was quiet. You could sense that the whole family knew what had happened and they expected something. They left the door open for the girl.

The next day you got up very early. The landlord greeted you kindly as before, but the awkwardness on his face confirmed your judgment, so neither of you looked at the other. At breakfast the girl didn't appear, and the landlord filled your bowl personally. His hand was trembling so that he spilt the porridge on the table. When you sent back the bowl to the kitchen later, you found the girl was there, cleaning the kitchen range surface that was already very clean. You could see only her back, but you could feel her cold face. After that, on many occasions such as on the way, or at the gate, as soon as she saw you she would turn her face immediately.

Looking at her pale face, you felt regret. It was very weird that just because of her ignoring you and hiding from you everywhere, you began to take an interest in her. You admitted to yourself that she was very pretty. Her charming face was just like the sun, and no matter where she went, men's eyes became sunflowers rotating around her. Besides, she was very smart, for she knew the real value of her beauty and had a high expectation for it, and she disdained those ordinary village guys. From people's talking you knew her name was Shuizhen, who was regarded as the most beautiful flower blossoming in this small village, Sujiagou. Nobody knew what kind of young man could get her, and when they talked about her they always gave you meaningful glances.

You knew they were talking about you and the girl, which was not a secret in the village, including that you—such an outstanding young worker from Beijing—lived at this most beautiful girl's home; including that both of you ignored each other and were cold to each other; and even including such a detail that the girl's eyelashes were quivering when she turned her face. All these had become meaningful topics for them to guess and mull over. You still looked calm when you walked in the village, but those looming gossips were just like a spider's web: though they couldn't fetter you, they couldn't be ignored either, because they, however invisible and untouchable, were lingering for you to disperse them. You could only hope that time would fade their memory—the two months' "guiding work" would be over soon, and after you left there, who would remember the relationship between a young guy from Beijing and a village girl, which might simply be a complete fiction.

The night before you left Sujiagou, when you went back to the landlord's home, you found the workshop director there. He sat on the *kang* facing the landlord, with Shuizhen sitting at the director's side. The director obviously drank a little, so he seemed very high. His face looked drunk and he put his handful of black hair on her shoulder. Shuizhen slightly lowered her head, one leg standing on the ground and the other hanging over the *kang*, and she looked as if she half-heartedly wanted to stay but might leave at any moment. When the door opened and you stood there, everyone looked up at you. You saw a trace of shadow and panic passing over Shuizhen's face, and she moved her body to get rid of the director's hand on her shoulder, but he held her tightly. You pretended not to notice this, and greeted the director without emotion then went to the back room to get some water. When you came out again, you found Shuizhen sitting on the *kang* entirely with both of her legs, and smiling at the director with that kind of shy and shining smile which you had seen before. You couldn't explain the reason that your heart felt a fierce hurt, as if a knife had stabbed it.

One month later, you didn't feel surprised when you met Shuizhen together with some other young women workers at the cement factory.

The darkness of night together with the smell of mosquito coils diffused through the room, and Dongzi and you sat on the bed side by side, smoking, with his butt sometimes burning, sometimes going out.

Dongzi said, "Even if you don't tell me, I can guess that it is you that Shuizhen really loves, and this is an open secret at this factory." He continued, "Only an idiot can't see. She makes jokes and flirts with all the other men except you, and as long as you are present she keeps silent. Even if she was fierce-looking one moment before, she becomes tame immediately like a rabbit. Once when you were talking with others, she listened attentively at your side, and you can't imagine how she looked at you."

He said, "You pretend you don't know what is happening, but actually everyone at this factory is clear about it, and several young guys even asked me to check with you whether you would want to give up Shuizhen to them."

You couldn't help laughing at their funny thoughts, for you and she didn't have any relationship at all. Dongzi agreed with you, sucking his cigarette fiercely. You asked how Shuizhen came to the factory and whether she had a fling with Wang Changhai, the bastard. Dongzi said between clenched teeth that Wang Changhai was really a bastard. Wang Changhai was the workshop director who went to the village with you before, and now he had become the factory director.

Like most men in northern Shannxi, this man had a lean body and a square face. This barren land—with its desolate highlands, its diet without any fat, every day's laborious tasks, as well as the genes inherited from their barbarian ancestors in the ancient times—bred such nice physiques which now we can only get at the gyms through a great deal of money and sweat. And as to the handsome appearance of a high nose and deep eyes, we can't get that no matter how much money we'd like to spend. Wang Changhai was outstanding among these high-nose and deep-eyes guys, and he could even be regarded as handsome, but you didn't think so, and you didn't know the reason either. He had a strong body, but the way he walked made you think of a swinging clothes rack. His eyebrows were black and his eyes were bright, but the smile at the corner of his month was a little gloomy and dubious, not noble or openhearted at all, which made the guy lose the handsomeness that should have belonged to him, just like a jade that lost its luster because of being covered by dust. Although men didn't like him, he was always appealing to women's eyes, which you couldn't understand completely.

You didn't know how Wang Changhai gave the opportunity of working at the cement factory to Shuizhen, but you were sure he definitely made some attempts on her affections. However, it seemed that he didn't succeed in the first several months, even in the first one or two years after Shuizhen entered the factory. Shuizhen was very cold to him and tried to keep her distance from him everywhere, which was quite obvious. For quite a long time Shuizhen was not among the many women around Wang Changhai, for she looked down her nose at the local workshop director, and instead more of her attention was on those groups of young workers from Beijing. While walking with other women workers on the newly finished road with poplars along it, most of those girls from the local countryside, Shuizhen was one of the most attractive. When a group of educated youths came from the opposite direction, her smile would become even more bright, which could strike all the men, and the educated youths were no exception. However, they were aware of what kind of determination they needed to really love a local village girl, so usually they just talked about her instead of taking action. Only the local young men among the many suitors had a real long-term goal, which Shuizhen was very clear about. In her bright smile there was always a little loss, a little depression, and a little disappointment, just like a blooming rose in the chilly November wind, lowering its head slightly though beautiful and blooming, but with a little melancholy and desolation, as if it had known that the warm sunshine was temporary and it was doomed to face the coming cold and frost, so its beauty was in vain. How couldn't people take pity on such a complicated beauty? And men could hardly resist such a beauty with such restraint, humbleness, weakness, and sadness.

You and she spoke very little. After she came to the factory, every time she met you on the way, she would bow her head immediately and start talking with other workers, pretending not to see you. You knew that she still took that matter to heart, but you didn't care, or in other words, you tried to appear that you didn't care. You believed that nobody at the factory knew what had happened between you and her in Sujiagou. Wang Changhai would never speak of it, even if he knew something about it, but the strange thing was that people's attention was still on you and her even after a long time.

Perhaps we should believe in the old saying that people's eyes are sharp.

Even now, you still remember clearly that afternoon one year after Shuizhen came to the cement factory. Wang Changhai had been the factory director at that time, and you had already left the dusty grinding workshop and were transferred to the laboratory for the quietest and easiest job in the factory. You were alone in the laboratory that afternoon, testing the compression index of a new furnace of cement. You didn't wear the thick uniform and dust-proof cap with protection flaps at the front and back side. You wore a doctor's overalls instead, because at the laboratory there was no dusty ore or huge noises except some equipment that attracted a lot of admiring looks although they were not expensive. The room was very quiet except for the weak sound of electric current from the machine. The pale yellow sunshine at noon gleamed on the pen in your hand while you recorded the data appearing on the dashboard, and the pen rustled when it touched the paper fixed on the board.

A subtle feeling made you turn around, and you saw her standing at the door. She was wearing dusty working clothes, with one hand wearing a glove and the other glove held in her hand. She was staring at you with her eyes wide open and her expression frozen, as if she had a nightmare or was conquered by some kind of magic. Your eyes met unexpectedly, and you saw a pair of dark black eyes full of pain, which you have never met since then in this world. They were as dark as an abyss without bottom, which swallowed all light, hope, and expectation. You were struck by the blackness, and your brain turned blank until the cement specimens behind you gave out a huge cracking sound, a heart-rending sound.

You hurried to pull down the electric brake, and when you turned around again there was nobody at the door. The sun at noon was shining on the empty doorframe. You couldn't tell if the eyes full of pain were your own illusion or reality. You had to restart the interrupted test, and you told yourself that was definitely nothing more than an illusion, for she was working at the workshop that was a few hundred meters away from you, and she had no reason to come here without permission. Moreover, the laboratory was too important a place to be entered into easily, while her workshop had very strict discipline. But on the other hand, what had happened just now was so true, living, and touchable. All those sights—the black, bottomless eyes, the painful expressions, as well as the glove being held in her hand—dirty, drooping, worn-out, with a hole at the fingertip—were not only vivid, but also distressing.

You didn't mention that afternoon to anybody. When you met her the next time, both of you dropped your eyes, and your eyes happened to be on that glove, the dirty and worn-out one, then you saw the hole at the fingertip, which made your heart tighten for an instant as if you were whipped, and you felt hurt. Now you and she had a second secret after that night at Sujiagou, which connected you two together no matter whether you wanted or not.

Several days after you told Dongzi about what happened at Sujiagou, when you went back to your dormitory, you were surprised to find that she was in your room.

The floor of the room was wet. It had been sprinkled with water and then swept. The messy quilt was neatly folded, the table and chairs were also very clean, and the windows were bright. On the table there was a plate of fried fish, which usually had been cooked by Dongzi and enjoyed by you only. Dongzi was talking to her happily, while she, sitting opposite him and smiling at him, with legs closed together, listened to him as attentively as a student. It could be found out that it was the first time for her to come here to be treated by an educated youth from Beijing, and the excitement and nervousness made her earlobes turn red. When you came in both of them looked up at you, and then one of them lowered her head while the other raised his head even higher. Your heart jumped several times and then became normal, for you didn't see that pair of worn-out gloves. She had changed her working clothes for a tidy outfit, and surely she wouldn't carry the old pair of gloves with her. This relaxed you for no reason, as if the secret between you and her also disappeared with that pair of gloves.

Dongzi looked at you with hostility, while you behaved at ease. You nodded at her calmly, for now she looked up again at you, and you took your washbasin and went out. You didn't come back to the dormitory until she left, but as soon as you entered the room, you slammed the door closed.

Dongzi sat on the bed alone, facing the wall, smiling as if the girl were still sitting squarely opposite him, and your anger didn't wipe the smile from his face.

You asked him, "What the hell are you doing?"

He looked at you with a smile at the corner of his mouth and told you that he liked her.

Your words were choked off and you became speechless. You went to your own bed, pulled off your shoes and clothes, and lay on your back looking at the ceiling, thinking over his words. But finally you were still speechless. Yes, what could you say? You should have found this out. You turned sideways, looking at Dongzi, who was still smiling, and you asked with a dry voice, "Are you serious?"

"Why am I not serious?"

"You have to think carefully."

"Nobody else thinks more than me."

After a while, Dongzi went to your bed and sat down, looking down at you. His face was red and his eyes were bright. "Hey, what do you want to say? Aren't you still thinking of her?"

"Fuck you!" Your voice sounded a little bit jealous, which made you feel very upset.

Then things started. Dongzi started to "date" her frequently, or to be exact, Dongzi thought that he was dating her. Every time she came, she would bring two or three other girls with her, sometimes even four or five girls, who were of course all village girls. Then a few young workers from Beijing who had slight interest in these girls also came for a gathering, and your room gradually turned to a real "urban and rural club." Usually a gathering with a group of young men and women couldn't bring about any actual development or result. They just sat around, talking and laughing, which could not only adorn a boring and dull life, but also avoid the inconvenience of separate dates. You were often not present on these occasions, and even if you were there when they came, you would leave with an excuse. They kept speaking and laughing without you, but your absence turned the smile on the girl's face more solitary. Time passed in this way, and everybody could see that Shuizhen was not really interested in Dongzi, and obviously she came happily for another purpose. You wanted to tell Dongzi the truth, for those local young guys looking on with a cold eye had already started to laugh at him, but you had been hesitating, because you were afraid of hurting him.

The rift between you and Dongzi erupted when you decided to move out of the dormitory. At that moment, both you and he felt very surprised at what happened.

That evening you were packing your things when Dongzi came back. You told him you decided to leave that room and move to another one. Dongzi asked you the reason, and you said he should have known but he said he didn't. He asked you if it was because he brought her to the dormitory. You laughed and told him that was not the reason because you had no feeling for that girl, and you decided to move out just because you wanted to have a quiet place. You said that you were not used to having so many people who you were not familiar with, or whom you didn't like, at the room every few days, and because of them you had to leave your own place and go to the other dormitory to read. You said that in this case, you'd better leave the room for him to enjoy freely. You had a quarrel. Dongzi insisted that you were jealous of him, while you laughed at him like a guy who likes eating shit, and then thinks all the people in the world like latrines. Finally, you two almost came to blows. Dongzi was so excited and angry that he threw a bowl to the ground and it broke into pieces, but you were determined to leave and you strapped up your box. However, you didn't expect that Dongzi would hug you when you went out the door.

Dongzi hugged you, and at that moment you were carrying the box with one hand, and one leg was already out the door. He held your waist in his arms tightly, and his hands formed such a strong ring around your belly that you couldn't get rid of them. His hands were cold, but his breath was hot, blowing on your neck with the moisture of tears, which you had never experienced before. He rested his head on your back, and as if speaking to himself, or whimpering, he said quietly, "You don't go! Please don't go! Don't go! Don't go!"

Both of you stood there motionless. Your blood coagulated, or to be exact, you were shocked because you didn't expect he could behave like this. You said to him, "Let me go. Let me go!"

Dongzi said, "Promise me you will not leave."

You sighed and with no other choice, you said, "OK, I am not leaving, but you must release me."

That night you two talked a lot, and also on that night you made a decision which would become your lifelong sorrow.

You don't know why you agreed to his absurd suggestion. Perhaps it was because of his tears that day, or because of his cold hands hugging your waist, or because of that long night when he poured out his life experience, which was very touching and became etched in your mind. Dongzi talked to you about his childhood in the *hutong* when he was crowded in the corner and beaten by other kids. His father fell from a high-tension cable and twitched into a mass of coke. His mother was always meek and bullied by others. His stepfather, FengBa, was an abominable guy. Dongzi told you that he looked down on women because of his mother. He said that women were just like animals. They made constant compromises in order to survive; they often suffered from being bullied or beaten; and they could only serve others with a fawning smile but without any dignity. He said only men could enjoy dignity and affection, but unfortunately, men usually just regarded violence and power as something important, and neglected their inherent capabilities. He said he felt very lonely, and in fact he had been lonely all the time. Then he said that when he met you, he immediately found the same loneliness on your face, and at first sight he was sure that you could understand him. He thought that he finally had a real brother when he saw how you treated Baba the dog. He said that he had been longing for a brother, and now you were his brother who hadn't appeared in the past twenty years. So he believed that you could understand him, and understand his feeling for that girl. He did want to stay here to live a life on the northern Shannxi Plateau as long as he could be together with the girl he liked and have a family of his own, which couldn't be found in Beijing but which could bring him warmth.

In the hazy night, you two had a long talk while smoking, and in the darkness only the shining butts from time to time, as well as the sounds, proved the existence of the other person. Even today you are still puzzled by his deep sound, full of feelings, and you feel such a sound and such a night came from a dreamland instead of life.

The next day was a Sunday. In the early morning, following your promise to Dongzi, you went to the riverside alone. You walked slowly along the river, which showed the clear ripples in the sunshine. You felt dizzy because of no sleep the night before and because of Dongzi's talk. That girl arrived at your side. You can remember clearly now that her hair was combed neatly and she wore a brand-new light blue Dacron outfit, and you had never seen her wear something so proper and neat. Her eyes were bright, looking at you happily and nervously.

She said, "Dongzi told me you invited me to come here." Her face turned even redder, and she bowed her head and asked in a low voice, "What's the matter?"

You said, "We are going to go to Qingliang Mount. Do you want to go? If you want, please don't take others." You emphasized "others" in your words, which she certainly noticed.

You arranged for a meeting at one o'clock in the afternoon at the hillside behind the Wanfu Cave, but you knew well that you wouldn't be there. Dongzi would be there instead.

In the evening, you were at the dormitory alone, waiting for him. You opened your favorite poetry, but you couldn't get into it. The verse you turned to was one from *The Book of Songs*:

> *I mount the southern hill green*
> *To gather thorn-ferns new*
> *While my lord can't be seen*
> *I'm full of grief and goo*

Such a kind of story took place in far remote, ancient times. It was about an infatuated lady and a hard-hearted man. The lady left home with the excuse of picking thorn-ferns, and she walked alone on the mount, carrying a small basket, the dew wetting her skirt and treetops messing up her hair. But where was the man who invited her, and who she would like to devote herself to and would rather have her body smashed into pieces for? The grass all over the mountains and plains just rustled; the sun rose and fell; the flowers blossomed and withered. How many times did they see the tears of such ladies! The girl wandering alone behind Qingliang Mount appeared in your mind. You closed the book and lay down on the bed, looking at the window. The moon looked nice that night. You felt vaguely that you did something wrong, but it was already irrevocable.

Still About Shuizhen

You slept some time that night, and when you woke up you found Dongzi wasn't back yet. You sat up, and while smoking a cigarette you considered whether you should look for him. You guessed something had happened, but it shouldn't take such a long time. You calculated in your mind that the round trip between the factory and the mount was less than five li, and even if they stayed there until dark it would take them less than an hour to come back. Furthermore, Dongzi left for there earlier than the appointed time, which was to say, when you met the girl at the river, Dongzi was already on the way to the mount. Even if the girl arrived later (in fact, this was impossible), they had the whole afternoon together, which should have been quite enough for them to express everything clearly. Why did they have to drag on late into the night?

You put on your clothes and went out.

The summertime in northern Shannxi was very cool, and although you put on your trousers, you still felt cold. The moonlight was just like water pouring over the hillside, caves, and stairs. The jujube trees cast dark shadows on the ground, quiet and soft, like a fairytale world. You walked down the long stairs in front of the cave and found one guy sitting there, and you knew it must be Dongzi. But from his motionless back you didn't know how long he had been there.

You went to him, stood opposite him, and you saw a white face which made you feel scared, for it was swollen, congestive, and livid. You didn't know at that time that actually you were seeing in advance the very face that would lay in the coffin among the flowers many years later.

You asked him what was wrong with him and why he didn't go back to the room and what had happened. His eyes were entirely black, shining with some weird light, and he murmured, "I fucked her."

Your heart beat a little, and then started to sink. A valve opened and the heart dropped heavily into it. You should do something…but you just sighed and sat beside him. You said feebly, "What are you talking about? You wouldn't have done that."

He said, "It's true. I really did. I fucked her. You don't believe me? You thought I wouldn't for the sake of you?" He

laughed quirkily. "I told you I did! I did! I did! Just at the
river, and I pressed her on the land. She cried. Do you know
how the bitch begged me? She begged me not to make her
clothes dirty, because they were borrowed from others. They
were borrowed! They were borrowed!"

You didn't know why you didn't raise your fist, and you
still don't know. Perhaps because the blood in your vessels
was doomed not to boil for anyone. Your blood could never
reach the temperature for boiling, which hadn't happened
before, and will never happen in the future. Perhaps the news
was too sudden for you to react. You just felt dizzy, so you
walked up the stairs with a roll, leaving Dongzi's crazy laughter behind. He staggered to catch you, looking more weak
and faint than yourself. Then he extended his hand for your
help, standing two stairs lower than you, just like a drowning
person stretching out his hand for rescue. You turned around
and took the hand but suddenly you stopped, maybe one second, maybe one minute. You, you and he—one was on an upper stair and the other on a lower one—looked at each other.
Then you purposely pushed him off the stair. Your strength
was so powerful that Dongzi fell on his back and rolled down
the stairs. His body was very weak and soft, and when the
different parts of his body touched the hard stones, they gave
out different sounds, while his posture was changing constantly, until finally it rolled another two times and stopped.
You just stood on the stair, watching. This was typical of you!
You wouldn't hit a person with your fist, but you could push
a person asking for help down the stairs. In the darkness, his
body curled up like a pile of mud, motionless. After a while
the mud moved, and a low and hoarse laughter sounded from
the darkness, like a snake that swallowed a frog, some part
narrow and some part wide, intermittently.

You turned around, went up the stairs, and came to the
door. You brought out the key to open the door, but you
couldn't put it into the lock. At last you opened it, went in,
felt for your bed, and sat down. You arched your body, with
your knees supporting your elbows and your hands covering

your face. You felt your head buzzing, and your hands shaking, which you couldn't stop.

The following is what Dongzi told you after he sobered up.

That noon, after Dongzi had waited a while at the hillside of Qingliang Mount, the girl arrived. She looked surprised when she found that only Dongzi was there. She asked why you didn't come, and following what you had discussed, he told her you had something to deal with and would come later. The girl believed him but with suspicion. Dongzi asked to take her to see the Qianfu Cave, but she didn't agree and said she had seen it before. Then Dongzi asked to take a walk on the mountain, but she insisted on staying there to wait for you. Dongzi tried to make conversation with her, but she replied only with much reluctance, absentmindedly. After about one hour, when Dongzi was thinking whether he should tell her the truth or not, the girl spoke first. She asked Dongzi whether you would come at all and whether you and Dongzi were acting in collusion to deceive her.

This shocked Dongzi, but he admitted the truth. Dongzi told you later that he regretted his reply. He said that actually he could find some ways to avoid the question or make up a new excuse. For instance, he could tell her that you might be delayed by something, or he could wait for you at the road or look for you with the girl together, but unfortunately, he was angered by the girl's coldness. He lost his mind. He felt humiliated. He said that he was just like a worm in the girl's eyes, but he was not a worm. He had a beautiful garden in his heart, where every flower blossomed only for her and where the sweet fragrance of these flowers was floating all around. They were swaying for her and offering their beauty for her, but she didn't see them; she refused to see them; she had no intention to see them. She stood up and went down the mountain, walking stiffly, like a statue made of clay.

Dongzi ran to her to grab her, which was his second mistake—he shouldn't have taken physical action, either to the desperate girl or to the desperate statue. Of course the girl struggled. She cried, and the sound was a horror and mournful, reverberating with tears in the silent hillside. The last little hope in his heart was broken by the cry, like the dew on the cobweb, which was very weak and fragile, dropped on the ground shakily. Even so, he didn't loose his hands, and he held the girl's hand tightly instead, as if he, being the dew, wouldn't fall down as long as he held her. But before he realized what was happening, he found he was surrounded by a group of angry persons who had rushed over, hearing her crying. They were local rural youths, and one of them knew the girl. Obviously, the girl's crying ignited their anger, so his hand was removed and the girl was released. Then they gave him a heavy blow to the face, which was so heavy that he felt his face was blasted with blood, and the ground before him turned over upwards. He staggered and almost fell, but the experience from gang war since childhood made him stand firm and give that guy a punch. He fell down immediately, but other guys behind rushed to him, and after several rounds Dongzi was knocked down. He curled up on the ground, surrounded by them, who kept kicking him from the left and right sides, just like the guy making fried fritters who kept rolling the fritters in the pan with chopsticks. The girl finally said, "That's enough. Let him go."

The girl went down the mountain with those guys, and Dongzi lay there alone for a while before he slowly rose up. His face was swollen, and he felt many lit torches were burning on his legs, his belly, and all over his body with his blood and muscle. He had never been beaten so ruthlessly, especially before a girl. The ground under him fell apart, and he not only fell from the fragile cobweb, but he also broke into pieces and became a plume of moisture swallowed up by dust. He staggered down the mountain and his only idea was how to find a group of the educated youths who would be willing to help him to take revenge. He didn't know whether he could find such persons, because he had no friends among those who were able to fight. You were his friend but you wouldn't fight for him, for you were not that kind of person by birth. While thinking of this, he couldn't help feeling a little desolate, and even harbored some resentment toward you. Why could you get everything without moving a finger, while he had nothing no matter how hard he tried? But at the moment he told himself that he could as long as he wanted. He carefully thought over the steps for revenge, including how to find the guy who took the lead. He didn't know the guy's name, but he thought he could be recognized easily for the girl was present and they knew each other.

He walked a while and then stopped a while since he felt faint, and when he struggled to the cement factory, looking at those caves, he realized he didn't want to go back to the dormitory, nor did he want to meet anybody, especially you, so he turned a corner in a trance and went to the river land. It was evening time and the place was very quiet; however, suddenly he found the girl standing there, at the very place.

Dongzi said, "I don't know why she didn't leave, or why she was standing there. Was she regretful and worried about me? Or was she there intentionally, watching me passing there and humiliating me one more time? But she was alone, in that large river land, which was unexpected. Then I went toward her, and in my mind the only idea was to take revenge. I must return the shame she forced on me."

It was dark everywhere in the cave. Dongzi's face covered with a towel looked weird. His changed voice because of pain, his swollen face, as well as the towel on his face, made him look strange in your eyes. You listened vaguely to him speaking intermittently, and from his incoherent narrative, you could clearly see the river land of that evening, where the water was flowing with the waves shining like fish scales under the sunset, as well as the girl standing there. Everything was so clear. Of course you knew why the girl went there. It was because it was there that you asked to meet her.

Dongzi said with a low and husky voice, "She called me bastard. She cried and called me bastard. Yes, I am a bastard, and I destroyed everything! All destroyed!"

Just as you had feared, the story of what happened that afternoon soon spread at the factory. The educated youth from Beijing and the local young workers belonged to two different groups from the very beginning at the factory, and now the rift which was implicit and hidden carelessly before was revealed openly and the two groups immediately became irreconcilable. What surprised you was that those educated youths who usually looked down on Dongzi now expressed great anger. They gathered at your room and discussed how to get the best compensation for Dongzi's swollen face, while those young village guys were also plotting revenge for their most beautiful girl's abuse. The plan of the educated youth was to beat fifty local guys and let their faces, as well as their legs and arms, become swollen also. (The guy who took the lead in attacking Dongzi definitely couldn't escape, and his name, as well as the identities of others who got involved in the fighting, were provided by a local educated youth who was an anonymous informer.) These youths eager for a fight planned all the details, such as the number of persons from each side (they were close, with the educated youths' side a little more); the abilities of fighting (through the training of violence, these urban educated youths were certain to have an upper hand); and the location and the timing. The only thing they didn't consider was the girl, for in everyone's eyes, she deserved punishment, which was just the least compensation for Dongzi's pain, and as to how much anger the girl's shame caused among the local persons who had been going after her, they didn't want to think about at all.

Among everyone, you had the most complicated feelings. You thought this account was hardly to be settled, for who could figure out the exact income and expenses in and out of the account? And who was the real winner and who was the real loser? For obvious reasons, Dongzi didn't mention the episode when you met the girl at the river that morning and your premeditation in advance, so in this case the meeting behind the Qingliang Mount became the girl's active invitation. The quarrel later was her not keeping her word, and the gang fighting Dongzi was even the premeditated unpardonable crime, which also became the reason why these educated youths were so angry. You wanted to tell the truth, but you hesitated because Dongzi didn't want to admit that he actively went after the girl (this is understandable, of course). Furthermore, deep in your heart, you didn't want to get involved in the matter, and you didn't want to face up to your innermost being either. After all, only you knew how much hurt the girl suffered.

Everyone on the road at the factory was at daggers drawn, and all the persons, both the educated youths and the locals, didn't walk alone anymore. They all walked in groups, with spades, long-handled wrenches, sticks, fluorescent tubes, and anything that could be used in self-defense or as an attack weapon. Every excursion might become a dangerous experience causing bloodshed, for nobody knew when and for what the fight would start. People were just like the cocks which were reddened to their cockscombs in a fierce cockfight, and they looked at each other with hatred. Fighting threatened to burst at any moment. However, just at this moment, the very moment, an unexpected thing happened: Wang Changhai got involved.

After that morning you met the girl at the river, she was the person you were most afraid to see. But in fact, after the matter, the girl disappeared and nobody knew where she went. It was after exactly five days that you saw her again. That day Dongzi was well and could walk by himself and it was time for working, so the educated youths crowded round him to go to work. To be exact, they thought it was time for them to take action. While they marched forth with Dongzi on the way, the other side must have realized this, for they also assembled together. Both sides were holding something at hand, which was really a spectacular scene. Now the two groups finally met. Of course, they had met many times before but this time the situation was different because this time Dongzi was present, which meant it was the real time to settle the score.

The sides were separated by fifty meters. Each group surveyed the other, anticipating the first word. It was very quiet, and such quietness with so many persons gathered together was frightening. That day was very bright, but the cloud of fight covered people's hearts. They were so devoted to staring at their opponents that nobody noticed that the iron door behind them, which usually donkeys went through to transport limestone, opened quietly, and a green Jeep drove in slowly. In the 1970s, cars were something rare, especially at a small cement factory in the countryside. But that day, when the road was crowded with people and a fight was about to start, the rare Jeep appeared. Today when you recall the matter, you can't help thinking that it was a deliberate arrangement.

That Jeep drove through the iron door slowly while people watched closely, and they made way for it to see it pass by slowly. It was driving very slowly, even slower than a person's steps, and the window of the Jeep was put down as if the persons inside it intentionally wanted both to clearly see the outside and to let the persons outside have enough time to see them. People outside did see the inside. Every place the Jeep passed by, the expressions on people's faces changed, with some whispering like wind blowing. Two names spread among them like ripples. The voice was weak but you got it, and you saw Dongzi standing beside you, shaking a little. Then, following other people's sight, you found the Jeep stopped in front of a two-storey brick building. The door opened. A tall man got out of it, walked to the other side of the Jeep, and pulled the door open. A girl emerged, whose back was toward us, and she lowered her head. Immediately there was a commotion among the people because all of them recognized her. They two, the man and the woman, under the public gaze, raised their heads and went into the building. That building was the office building where the factory director's office was located. People kept silent and both sides of the fight gazed at each other in speechless despair. Then it seemed someone gave a soundless signal, and people scattered. The two groups became demoralized, and the persons mixed together and disappeared everywhere in the factory, scattered like sand.

An upcoming fight was cancelled by an abruptly appearing Jeep, and it was cancelled so quickly and completely it was just as a drop of water falling into sand. All the people at the cement factory saw clearly that the man sitting in the Jeep, looking at them with his highly deterrent eyes, was their director, Wang Changhai. The woman, the Helen who caused this Trojan War, was Shuizhen.

You called her a woman, because you found out, actually all the persons found out, that from that day on there was no more girl called Shuizhen, but there was another person who was also called Shuizhen, only she was not a girl, but a woman instead.

Wang Changhai

Different from what we learned in books, many places in the countryside might be limited, but they weren't feudal at all. Very young girls and boys heard vaguely in their dreams the sounds made by their parents sleeping on the same *kang* with them; then from those unrestrained and amorous behaviors of animals in the fields, they knew the secret of life and experienced it themselves in haystacks, cattle pens, or small ravines. When they grew up and finally married their own wives or husbands, on those nights without lightbulbs or TVs, that thing would naturally become the only fun to be enjoyed by themselves or shared with others. But you would never expect that such an activity would be staged during the daytime like a show. When the sky was clear and the sun was shining, the guys, tired of planting, would put down their hoes for a rest, then some red-faced, sweaty women would scream, yell, and run excitedly in groups, and they would catch a prey that they took a fancy to. They would wrestle him to the ground, pull out his penis, and make concerted efforts to let it ejaculate ardently. This should have happened secretly in an obscure hairdresser's parlor or an underground brothel, but now to your great surprise, it was carried out in broad daylight, with people laughing and watching, and even with their joint participation. Because it was open and public, it became innocent; because it was accepted by all of them, it became legal. It was more a game than a ritual, and the name of the game was "cutting rafter," which was only one word different from the innocent kids' game called "cutting sandbag." The guy to be cut might be a newly married husband, a stableman, a scorekeeper, or even a village head and a team leader, but the first criterion was that he must be a married man. (They didn't cut the unmarried, single men, perhaps because of the unique sense of morality in the village or perhaps because of some old taboo.) No wife turned angry when her husband was cut in public because she herself might cut other women's husbands. Both sides of cutting and being cut reached a balanced state of mind on account of the equality of offer and reward. Moreover, perhaps in their minds, their husbands' becoming prey reflected their own great charm.

Just as you guessed, when he was young, Wang Changhai was the most popular "rafter" and he was cut most frequently in the village, which he told you proudly one night when you two went to Sujiagou together. That day you and he went to the field and happened to see the very scene. You saw those women bending down to busy themselves doing that thing, some men beside them smiling with pipes in their mouths, as well as the girls whispering with their faces flushing in the far distance. Wang Changhai gave you a look and found you were at a loss for not understanding what was happening, then he smiled meaningfully, which showed that he was in a commanding position because he knew some secret that you didn't. People scattered because you and he arrived, and a man full of dust with disheveled hair and a dirty face stood up, with his hands carrying his trousers. Wang Changhai shouted in a very high voice, "Why stop? Keep cutting!"

Those women laughed, and a fat one looking like the head of them stood out and said, "No good rafter! Do you have one?"

Wang Changhai laughed heartily. "I have a rafter you can never cut down!" His obscene gestures brought everyone even happier laughter. From then on you didn't go to the field anymore, for you knew the smartest way not to disturb this kind of happiness was to avoid it.

You were promoted to group leader of the workshop after coming back from Sujiagou. A few months later when he became the factory director, you were transferred to the lab, which was the only job in the factory where one didn't have to swing a sledgehammer or wear a dust-proof mask, and which was also the only job without the regulation of working on three-shift. So obviously this was a reward for your behavior in Sujiagou when you were with him. You were tight-lipped and had no curiosity—or, to be exact, you were good at pretending to be ignorant, which was what Wang Changhai appreciated most in you. But maybe that was not the only reason, and the core of your subtle relationship with him was elsewhere.

The abrupt appearance of the Jeep opened a new chapter in the life at the cement factory. You had to admit that Wang Changhai's manner was really very imposing and decisive, which shocked all the people and also made them utterly convinced. People usually strongly condemned furtive adultery, but were at loss for words about the blatant cohabiting. Moreover, this act could be referred to as "the hero rescuing the beauty." Moreover, the background of the matter was power, with his imposing manner as its support.

As to how Wang Changhai got Shuizhen, or in other words, how Shuizhen sought refuge with Wang Changhai, the huge tree, for shelter, there were several versions. One version was that at that night Shuizhen herself went to the factory director Wang Changhai's dormitory. Wang Changhai had a family, but everyone knew that his frail wife, with his three sons, was seeding the fields with corn in his hometown around a hundred li away from the factory. Therefore, being a man, Wang Changhai felt very lonely. His dormitory was not with those for the workers, but instead was kept only for himself on the second floor of the office building, next to his own office. However, his dormitory was not unfamiliar to others because he often mixed his office up with his dormitory, and he liked to invite young women workers to talk about work in his dormitory or to play cards with men in his office during the whole night. That night Shuizhen was lucky, for the director was playing cards with men. If he had been talking work with another young woman, her fate might have been different. According to an insider's information, Wang Changhai's luck was not good at that moment: a succession of goods cards were outdone by others, and he was holding the king, wrestling, for he was indecisive about whether he should keep it to the last or play it now for getting some scores first. Then the girl appeared, her eyes swollen after too much crying.

Since she appeared behind Wang Changhai, several other men at the office saw her first, and there was no doubt that they all were greatly surprised by the miserable condition of the most beautiful girl in the factory. They found that her eyes were red and swollen, her clothes were messy, and she was breathless. These men said that she looked like she was "waiting charmingly to be fucked again after being fucked." They looked straight at her, forgetting to play their cards, which prompted Wang Changhai's attention, so he turned around and saw the girl. It was said that everything in the office, including the air, was motionless for a few minutes, and all the persons were looking forward to the coming commotion with the inevitable gloat. But Wang Changhai really deserved to be a director: it took him only one minute, maybe only a few seconds, to make a clear judgment on the situation. He stood up at once and said, waving his hand decisively, "The meeting is over," as if he were really holding an important meeting instead of playing cards. One poker buddy protested in a low voice that the director stopped the game just because he himself was not lucky at cards. Usually such a comment would bring the guy thunder-like roars, but things were different that day, so our director tolerated the disrespectful words and smiled confidently. "Young guy, I tell you I am sure to have the biggest luck in my whole life tonight." All the men could understand his implication, and they filed out with meaningful and obscure smiles. At the door, they looked at the girl again for a long time before they left reluctantly. Although they were reluctant, they had to leave, for they knew that at this critical moment they should restrain themselves for their own good.

Before going downstairs, the last one to leave asked, "Should I lock the building door for you?"

Our director gazed on the girl and cursed loudly. "Why would you lock the door? We are working!"

Another version similar to this one was like this: when she appeared, she didn't look so miserable. She was tidy and clean without any sadness of being humiliated, but looked calm and ready to sacrifice instead. She impressively appeared before these muddle-headed, dispirited men immersed in smoke, smelly feet, and the choice between spades K and hearts A. She knocked at the door fearlessly and said sternly, "Director, please come out." In this version, Wang Changhai was sitting facing the door, so when he raised his head he immediately saw the girl standing at the door, whose face lit up his face like fire in the dimness. He threw away the cards at once and ran out, his eyes shining, and when he was running, unfortunately he hit his leg on the chair but this didn't impede him from disappearing from these men's sight in the shortest time. Nobody knew what they talked about, and those men in the office at that time took the opportunity to peep at the director's cards placed upside-down on the table, which meant at that moment their concerns about their own financial benefits temporarily surpassed their concerns about sexual relationships.

The director came back before they had time to go back to their own seats but, strangely, he didn't show any anger about their furtiveness. Instead, he smiled to announce the meeting was over, which made those who peeked at his cards feel very disappointed for they thought they lost a chance to make a small fortune. Someone who was dissatisfied made the comment about luck, and then our director said with a confident smile, "Young guy, I tell you I am sure to have the biggest luck in my whole life tonight."

Of course, there was the third version, in which it was the director instead of the girl who went to see the other. It was said at that moment the girl kept crying and sobbing for her misfortune in her dormitory, with several female companions comforting her, and then her destiny knocked at the door—Wang Changhai appeared. His high body covered the dim light in the cave, and his solemn steps shocked everything and everyone. He went to Shuizhen under the others' gaze, looking dignified, and reached out his hand to the crying girl. The girl looked up, their eyes met, and then she grabbed the big hand like in a dream. She stood up and followed him to go out. All the persons present were dumbfounded. They didn't say anything during the whole process—nothing, not a word. All happened in silence: he went into the cave, went to her, and reached out his hand. She raised her head, looked in his eyes, and grabbed the hand. There was no need for words; they seemed redundant. And the implication behind these actions was too rich and huge to be expressed by words at all. Another related version from this one was that those female companions didn't remember to check where they went until they already left, so the girls ran outside the cave, looked down from the stairs, and saw the Jeep, which meant Wang Changhai was driving a Jeep to pick up Shuizhen.

Many years later when you recalled the several different versions, you realized that the first and second versions should be from men, because they implied men's fantasy that a woman who they had long coveted would throw herself into their arms; the third and fourth ones should be from women, because they showed those Cinderellas at that cement factory had a strong desire for finding favor with Wang

Changhai, the director, the powerful emperor. But in fact all these versions were imaginary, and mixed with the feelings of the creators, which were quite far from the real facts. The truth was nobody knew how Shuizhen and Wang Changhai went together. Their first appearance was with that Jeep, and you had to admit that was a wonderful scene, for both its time and its location were chosen carefully, which displayed too many meanings and solved too many problems, and which also calmed down all commotion and restlessness. So in comparison with the role it played, the truth and the process were of no importance.

Why didn't Wang Changhai take revenge on Dongzi with his power? The reason would be mentioned later.

Just now you said that life at the cement factory had a new chapter, and the reason was certainly Shuizhen. After the Jeep appeared, the girl called Shuizhen before disappeared or was lost, and a woman called Shuizhen replaced her. The biggest difference between the girl called Shuizhen and the woman called Shuizhen was the former was like a shy and small kindling buried deep under the ground, waiting for others to ignite it. The latter was like a wildfire spreading on the ground, making trouble everywhere. Now when Shuizhen walked on the way to the factory recklessly, she flirted with all men with her shining eyes. She became such a woman that she had already violated and killed all men in her heart, and her eyes, her mouth, her words, as well as her unbridled body language, all proved this. Her outstanding beauty turned into lightning, burning anyone she chose, so one would be burnt with the slightest negligence. Countless men were burnt by her, one by one, including the workshop director, the army representative, and ordinary boiler men. Some of them were burnt by accident, while others drew fire against themselves willingly.

To all these happenings, Director Wang Changhai just gave a tolerant and confident smile, which taught you to understand the local persons' broadmindedness to sexual relations. Two years later Wang Changhai brought his wife to the factory, and when the director of tall and large stature walked arm-in-arm with his old wife of short and frail figure, everyone witnessed the couple's close relationship and deep feeling. It was said that Shuizhen was among the women workers who greeted them, and her respect to the director's wife was definitely no less than those who once went to the director's dormitory to discuss work. This was life. Many years later, when you passed the cement factory on a business trip, you met the retired director, Wang Changhai, and you heard that Shuizhen had two sons and turned fat and became a good wife and mother. You also heard that Wang Changhai's wife was dead and Wang Changhai bought her an expensive cemetery and reserved his own grave beside hers, with their two names engraved on the tombstone.

Now we should talk about Dongzi, who was the real hero of our story.

The person who really felt sad for Shuizhen was Dongzi, and you knew clearly that only he truly liked Shuizhen, and he not only liked her, but also regarded her as his puppy love. When the gossip about Shuizhen and Wang Changhai was in a hubbub at the factory, and when the people took great delight in talking about the girl who had become a constant topic of love affairs and the center of scandals, Dongzi lay in the cave with his eyes wide open one night after the other. He sighed, and asked himself, *How can women change so quickly?*

One time an educated youth talked of Shuizhen. He said that it was Dongzi who, on behalf of the educated youths in the cement factory, first opened the great Suez, and after that all other ships, whatever their sizes, shapes, or tonnages, just followed the old channel to perform a routine. His words originally intended to please Dongzi, but annoyed him instead. He took a mug and threw it at the guy, which shocked everybody.

Only you could understand his pain, so when the following thing happened, you didn't feel surprised at all.

At noon, you just went back to the dormitory after finishing the early shift, and as usual you were taking a sponge bath behind a curtain when you heard some sound at the door. You thought it was Dongzi, so you didn't turn around and you continued to dry your body and put on your shirt, but when you turned around while putting on your clothes, you were suddenly dumbfounded, for you saw Dongzi with that woman standing at the door.

Both you and he didn't say anything for several seconds. You never expected those two would appear together on this occasion, at this moment, and moreover, you weren't dressed yet. But the condition of that woman was no better than yours: half of her body and both her hands and legs were covered with dirty black mud, that kind of fermentative mud which could only be found in newly fertilized vegetable fields. The stench coming from the black mud instantly pervaded your small room, which made your embarrassment manifest. But Dongzi didn't care about your embarrassment at all, and he just poured the half bucket of water (which you left for him) into the big tub he used for taking a sponge bath, put the towel and soap at the ready, and pulled up the curtain. He asked the woman to go behind the curtain for a bath. The woman hesitated for a moment, and then proudly went behind it while you turned around and hurried to dress yourself.

The woman took a bath behind the curtain with the gurgling sound of water, while Dongzi and you sat outside wordlessly.

You later understood the situation. On the way home after work, Shuizhen encountered a group of women workers by chance, and they quarreled for no known reason, although it was surely something trivial. The location of their quarrel happened to be beside a pond for storing compost, therefore the outcome of this quarrel was obvious. After a few words clashed between them, Shuizhen was pushed into the pond. It was said that only one woman quarreled with her, but at least four or five women pushed her into the pond, and she fell before she could offer resistance. Luckily, the pond for storing compost was not deep and it only covered her knees.

She protected her face from being stained with the help of one arm, otherwise the result would have been terrible. The troublemakers had left by the time she started to climb out of the pond. It seemed that nobody helped her although more than ten people were watching. At last she came out and walked to her own dormitory under the public gaze. More than a dozen onlookers followed her indifferently, and because of the smell and other well-known reasons, they kept their distance from her. (It looked like a sparse parade.) Then Shuizhen went to the door of her dormitory, half of her body covered with black mud. The door was not locked but it couldn't be opened, so she knocked on it. She wanted to clean herself after she went in, but nobody opened the door for her. (Her roommate explained later that she wasn't in, although many persons saw the door fastened from inside.)

At this time, more and more onlookers were gathering. Shuizhen knocked on the door several times without an answer, and then she shouted many times without a response. Finally, she pounded vigorously, but the door was impassive. She turned back and looked at those onlookers, who then took two steps back to make the circle surrounding her even larger. But when she turned again to the door, they gathered closer again. This time she didn't look back, and she leaned her forehead on the door and lowered her head as if she were asleep. People looked at her intently, just watching the girl whose body was half-covered with smelly black mud helplessly leaning against the door. Time passed, one second after another, and then it stopped. After maybe several minutes, or several hours, or even several years, they found the girl was crying. Her shoulders were moving and jerking with repressed sobbing, and she made faint sounds as if from a small animal.

You imagined that it was at this moment that Dongzi stepped forward. He went out of the onlookers and to the girl; he patted her shoulder. Shuizhen turned around and saw his eyes and also saw his extended hands. Then she held the hands.

Indeed, you didn't know how Dongzi took Shuizhen back to your dormitory. You didn't know how Dongzi, with the woman, passed those onlookers and those gazes. You didn't feel surprised at the attack the woman suffered—to such a woman as Shuizhen, to fall prey to such a plot planned by other women was not surprising at all. What surprised you was why Dongzi happened to see it, and why he could extend his hands which were impossible to be refused at such an opportune time and place.

The sound of water came from behind the curtain constantly, and you felt that a long time passed. Neither you nor Dongzi said anything in the depressing state. Maybe because the woman was present, neither of you had the intention to talk. When the sound of water stopped, suddenly Dongzi remembered something and asked you in a low voice whether you had some clothes. "What clothes?" You didn't understand his question. Dongzi's face turned red and he said, "Clothes for her to put on, clean clothes." You asked him why he didn't give his own clothes to her, and he told you that his were dirty, they weren't washed yet. You didn't ask anymore and stood up to find something of yours. Dongzi's face turned redder as he passed your clothes to the woman through a gap in the curtain.

Then the woman emerged from behind the curtain wearing your things, which were clearly too big for her, but on the other hand, you found she had a distinctive flair wearing the oversize clothes. Holding her own dirty clothes, she asked Dongzi to give her an old newspaper in which to wrap them. Dongzi gave her a canvas bag instead, and she said that was not proper, for her clothes would make the bag dirty. Dongzi hurried to say that it didn't matter at all, and then he said it again. He reassured her that the bag was useless to him and he hurried to put her clothes into it in case she would refuse it. His behavior made you feel embarrassed. The woman smiled, one hand smoothing her wet hair, and she said in a low voice, "You are good guys."

Her gentle words evoked in both of you infinite emotions, and suddenly a kind of warm feeling surged into the air, as if the time were back to that innocent period when she just came to the factory. Dongzi stared at the white and clean part behind her ear, and to him she really became more captivating after taking a bath, which the woman certainly realized. She also knew whose clothes she was wearing. (You once wore that shirt at Sujiagou.) She gave you an oblique glance and a meaningful smile, her face blushing. She said, "How should I thank you?" While speaking, she unfastened one button at the chest with her fingers, as if unintentionally.

You could hear Dongzi's gasping immediately, and his body shook as if he couldn't stand still. The woman giggled, went to the door, and asked, "Which of you wants to walk a little way with me?"

Dongzi involuntarily followed her to the door, but you grabbed him by the arm. The woman saw this, laughed more loudly, and then she disappeared.

Dongzi was still shaking, with his teeth chattering. You embraced his shoulder without any words, standing in the room. And you two stood there just like this, motionless, for quite a long time.

Then there came those absurd days, which were unreal and unreasonable days in your memory. They lasted perhaps a few days, half a month, or a few months, but for you, how long it lasted was not important at all. What was important were the mixed feelings between reality and dream that those days left in your heart. You couldn't distinguish how much was real and how much was just a dream.

Such days started one night when you found Dongzi was not in his bed and not in the room either when you woke up. You got up to look for him and found him walking back along the road from the empty factory, his face livid, and the expressions in his eyes lost. You didn't know whether he was sleepwalking or suffering some attack. Another time when you woke up, you found Dongzi was sitting on his bed dazedly, his body full of dust and the bruising scars on his forehead proving that he went out when you fell asleep and had some physical clash with others. Vaguely you thought you knew what had happened and you asked him, but he kept silent and just lay down to sleep. When you found the second and the third sets of scars on his face, you were determined not to stand by anymore. That night as usual you turned out the light and pretended to go to sleep, but you listened carefully to his movements. Around midnight you heard him getting up, putting on his clothes lightly, pulling open the door, and going out. Then you followed him, and you found him walking very fast, striding forward. He looked and walked straight, as if he were being led by an invisible rope. The moonlight in the clouds appeared from time to time, and there was nobody on the road by the factory. He passed along the long road and went to the two-storey brick building. The light was still on upstairs, and you knew the light was from Wang Changhai's office. Dongzi held the handle of the building door to shake it. The door was apparently locked from the inside and supplemented by an iron bar which, under Dongzi's shaking, clanged back and forth, and gave out hoarse screams in the silent night. Dongzi went two steps back, then rushed forward to violently kick the door with his foot. After being attacked, the door moved backward, and the iron hinge with an iron lock hanging on it seemed rickety but they were still tightly pulled together like a pair of lovers hard to part. Dongzi stopped after kicking several attempts, took a deep breath, raised his head to look at the sky, and suddenly sang loudly, "The east wind is blowing; we are beating the drum. In today's world, who is more afraid in the end?"

His out-of-tune roar reverberated in the darkness as shrill as a wild wolf. After singing for a while, he gave the door another kick as if it were an accompaniment, then he continued his singing. As a result, the hoarse, metallic sound mixed with his out-of-tune roar was particularly loud in the dark, empty night, and swept the whole factory area like a strong wind. It is no exaggeration at all to describe it as earth-shattering. When you were wondering how people's hearing was so slow, the window upstairs opened and a man leaned out of it to look down. This was Director Wang Changhai, who shouted while looking around, "Feng Dongzi, I know it's you! If you keep making trouble, I will inform the security section to catch you and put you into the prison! I will do what I say!"

Dongzi looked up and asked, "Where is she?"

Wang Changhai then asked, "Who? Who are you asking about?"

Dongzi kept kicking the door, and continued his singing in his rusty voice, "We people aren't afraid of the American imperialists, but instead they are afraid of us."

Wang Changhai laughed, "You are mad! She is not here! I can swear to Chairman Mao that she is not here! Go find her elsewhere!"

Dongzi stopped both his voice and his foot and turned around to go elsewhere, while you were dumbfounded, hiding in the shadow of the grove. You didn't know when Dongzi started such an absurd game. Did he lose his mind? From the reply of Wang Changhai, you could make the judgment that this was not his first time behaving like this, and he had been punished. (The scars on his face were the evidence.) Maybe the game and the punishment had happened many times. Everyone in the factory knew about it except you!

Your stomach knotted at this realization, and you determined to follow him. Now Dongzi was walking forward along the road and, as you expected, before him was the gate to the women's dormitory, but just at this moment several shadows appeared and they blocked him. They had sticks in their hands, and you heard Dongzi's out-of-tune voice again. "The east wind is blowing; we are beating the drum." But his voice was interrupted by some muffled sounds, because those black shadows swung the sticks and Dongzi was swallowed up. You realized what happened and you took one stick from the pile of stakes on the ground and rushed up with loud screaming. After some fierce fighting, the black shadows escaped.

Dongzi sat on the ground, his head in his hands, and then you helped him walk back slowly. The cool wind was blowing, and you helped him walk back slowly on the road. If someone came from the opposite direction at that moment, he would have seen us, two educated youths covered in dirt, one wearing very thin clothing and the other with wounds on his head. The leaves on the poplars on each side of the road gave out sounds as if whispering or sighing; a yellow leaf dropped from a branch during one sigh and whirled down in front of you.

That autumn night will stay in your memory forever, for it was on that night that you, helping Dongzi, walked on the road by the factory. The night was quiet, with dark blue stars in the sky. The leaves were yellow, like golden tin foil stuck on the night background. The white road looked endless, and you two just walked, walked, and walked. But then what did you see? Above your heads in the sky, those stars suddenly grew long feathers.

Yes, they had shining long feathers, piece by piece, root by root, shining and flying in the dark blue night sky. And the core of these shining feathers, which was next to stars, was a white color, which then became light yellow, light red, light purple, and then it became heavy, then light again, and without clear boundaries it melted with the whole night. The stars were quite close to us and looked very low, just hanging over your head, up and down as if moving, and left and right as if floating, which made them look like living things. These huge, crystal, cold stars looked as if they were breathing, shaking, floating, and smiling.

Dongzi murmured, "The stars have feathers."

You agreed, "Yes, feathered stars."

But it was quite probable that this didn't happen on that night, but on another night when you crossed the Qinghai-Tibet Plateau. Because it seemed you didn't walk on the road by the factory, but another much quieter one, a higher altitude one, which was lying on the roof of the world, and where the air was as cold as ice. It was a totally lone and silent wilderness, without anybody to be found. The front was quite remote and the road was endless. Only the shining snow, the clean and white brightness peculiar to the mountain, was waiting for us in the far distance.

More probably it just happened in your dream, for in fact you passed the Qinghai-Tibet Plateau by truck, and you remember you didn't get off the truck that night. But there were too many such nights which overlapped and appeared in your dreams in disorder after Dongzi died.

The next day you asked for leave to take Dongzi to see the doctor. The expressions on the doctor's face were so complicated that you couldn't guess what he was thinking, and he just applied some mercurochrome to the wounds. You were sure that in less than ten minutes the whole factory would spread the story about Dongzi's new scar, and you were also sure that the length of the scar would have an exponential growth directly proportional to the length of the story. But you were unable to interfere with these things, and you could only take care of what you could. For instance, you couldn't control people's tongues or imaginations, but you could control Dongzi's legs. Coming out of the clinic, you didn't go to the workshop but instead went toward the dormitory with Dongzi. He asked you to go to work, but you told him you wouldn't and that you had asked for leave for three days. Dongzi didn't speak anymore. You prepared many newspapers and a few magazines for him, and you stuck close to him. You cooked for him, helped him to wash his face with clean wet towels, and even washed his feet for him. You picked up the quilt he kicked off to the ground and you tucked him in. You took the noodles you cooked to his bed. The first day he was cooperative; the second day he said your cooking was not good; and the third day he even said that your cooking was just like shit and he poured the porridge into the urinal. You didn't say anything. You simply picked up the bowl and cleaned it. You latched the door and sat by the lamp to read. Dongzi looked at you with a sarcastic expression, coughed loudly, and then spat on the table, but you just silently wiped it up with paper. Next, he put ashes into your cup, which you pretended not to see. Finally, he jumped up and rushed to the door, while you immediately outstripped him and blocked the door. He pushed you, but you were immovable. He grabbed your arm to pull you away, but you held the door handle tightly. At last, he struggled with you and you two were just like two wrestling bulls. Dongzi abruptly clung to your waist and threw you onto the ground with his leg, and before you could react, he punched you in your face heavily.

Dongzi yelled, "Why the fuck are you blocking me? Why are you blocking me? You are a bastard! An arrogant bastard! Who do you think you are? Just because you are superior, because you are more intelligent, handsome, and popular than me, because she likes you, and everybody likes you, then I have to obey you? I tell you, you are a bastard! An asshole! A shit! I will not listen to you! Why should I listen to you? Why? Why? Why?"

Dongzi growled hysterically, spittle at the corner of his mouth, his face distorted with anger, looking very ugly and strange. You got up, silently wiped the blood from your month, and went forward to Dognzi. All of sudden, you struck back at his mouth with your fist, and he fell down.

You panted, pointed to his nose, and said word by word, "Just for this!"

Dongzi lay on the ground, his eyes closed, breathing without motion, blood running from his nose, while you stood there looking at him and panting. When you wiped the blood on your mouth, your palm became red immediately and you could taste the blood in your mouth. You felt very sick, so you angrily spat the spittle with blood on Dongzi's face. The spittle with blood dropped straight onto Dongzi's cheeks under his eyes, half-red and half-white, shining and falling down along his swollen cheeks, stopping at the corner of his mouth. You looked at the spittle bewilderedly, as if it were a living thing. You found it was creeping, and Dongzi must have felt this also, for he seemed to experience it with his eyes shut. Then you saw a small detail, an action not easy to be noticed: he stuck out his tongue to lick the spittle which was still dripping down slowly, and the red tip of his tongue looked like a small hand which stuck out quickly and then withdrew. You were astonished. The action was so abrupt and tiny that you had no time to savor its meaning.

Just this moment Dongzi laughed, lying on the ground with his eyes still shut and his body huddled up, and he laughed with twitches, as if an invisible hand were pulling the sinews through his whole body with a rhythm of loosening and tightening. Dongzi rolled over by the invisible pull from one side to the other, and then rolled back, and he was laughing all the time until his throat became hoarse and his eyes welled over with tears. He said breathlessly, "Salty. It is salty."

You looked at him laughing and, surprisingly, you then understood his meaning and you laughed too. You couldn't understand why you laughed with him, but you kept laughing, with your body leaning against the wall for support until finally you sat on the ground beside Dongzi, laughing with him together. You two laughed uncontrollably.

Suddenly, Dongzi embraced you and then pressed himself on your body. The laughter stopped. You, and Dongzi himself, were shocked by his action and you two looked at each other in extreme astonishment. Dongzi's face, with your spittle and blood, half-red and half-swollen, looked very weird and now it turned even redder. From your vision, his face looked much bigger than usual. He leaned his red face to you, and you could sense his breath on your face. His hand softly touched the bloodstain at the corner of your month, and said tenderly, "I am such a bitch."

His voice was very weird and very low, with tenderness you were not accustomed to. His eyes were bright with something watery shining inside, which somewhat scared you. You remembered his tongue sticking out and then withdrawing just now, and immediately you felt very sick, so you pushed him aside and stood up.

"You are really a bitch," you said in a casual way on purpose to cover your uneasiness. You kicked him with your foot, crossed from his body, and went away.

After this abnormal experience, you started to think over how to separate from him. Then you made the decision to leave him. You knew this undoubtedly would be very cruel to Dongzi at that stage, but you told yourself that you had already done too much for him, yes, too much, which inevitably made him indulge in fantasy. Among the young workers at this cement factory, there was no lack of certain pairs. That Dongzi must have had some desire for you was becoming more and more obvious, while you were already tired of this kind of relationship. You knew that you and he were two kinds of persons, and actually you had known before you were different from him, just as you were different from the girl. You told yourself that it was not your fault that those who were quite different from you treated you well. You were doomed to separate, sooner or later, and in this case, why didn't you separate now? As a result, though sometimes you blamed yourself inwardly, you carried out your plan in a low key.

You began to treat him indifferently, tried to annoy him with words, and you even found another worker to play table tennis to replace him. Considering that Dongzi once strongly prevented you from moving out, you knew the best way was to let him ask to move away. You were sure he couldn't stand you longer than a few days because of his bad temper. It turned out that your relationship became cold soon. His face looked displeased, and he didn't know for what reason he annoyed you, and you didn't give him any chance when he wanted to check with you. Now it was you, instead of him, who spent most time out of the dormitory. You even hoped that he would go to look for the girl (the woman) again, and if so, you would not prevent him or save him anymore, then he would realize that you would not look for him and help him.

However, it was very strange that Dongzi seemed to see through your plan, so instead he didn't go out anymore, but was determined to stay in the room waiting for you, which was somehow out of your expectation. One day he blocked the door when you prepared to go, and you two had a bitter quarrel, which was the most serious one since you lived together. During the quarrel, he broke your fishing rod and without any hesitation you smashed the electric furnace for cooking. Finally, Dongzi asked to break up and you calmly accepted. But just when both of you agreed that no matter who found the house first, he would move out, Dongzi had an accident.

You always think that the accident happened on purpose, or in other words, it was plotted deliberately. There was a hanging pot in Dongzi's workshop, which was used for holding the smashed lime ore. Usually this pot was supported firmly by a stand, but on that day the stand suddenly collapsed and the hanging pot dropped while Dongzi was standing under it to take a sample from the limestone to send it to the lab. Everybody knew that Dongzi was usually in charge of collecting the ore samples. One of his legs was broken by the pot. When you got there after hearing the news, the ambulance had already arrived. Lying on the stretcher, his face was as pale as a piece of white paper. You held his hands, feeling heartbroken. You didn't tell anybody else that indeed you should have come to collect the sample that day because, one day before this incident, the new regulations were just announced that the lab technician was supposed to come to the workshop in person to collect the sample, so that was as if to say that the accident was originally plotted against you.

That night you went back to the dormitory and found in your case the dagger which you brought back one year before when you went to Tibet for vacation with Dongzi. A green jade was embedded in its curved handle, and a groove was engraved on its straight blade, which was for blood to flow through. You calmly took the dagger out from the bottom of the case, pulled out its blade, and held it under the light. The bright blade under the light was swaying, just as ice and snow were pouring down and flowing down along the hillside with avalanche sounds. But maybe it wasn't ice and snow; maybe it was your heartbeat instead. You closed your eyes and Dongzi's face full of blood appeared before you. You couldn't get rid of the thought that your idea to abandon him ruined him. You opened your eyes, and the sound of the avalanche was over. It was quiet everywhere. You put other things back into the case and locked it, and then you rolled up your bedding and tied it with a string. You wrote your family address in Beijing on a piece of paper, and put the paper on the table shared by you and Dongzi. Finally, you put the dagger into your pocket and went to the door. When you turned off the light, you looked at the room again with nostalgic eyes. You and Dongzi had lived there for such a long time. You thought with much pity that if there were not this accident, perhaps Dongzi would be collecting his own belongings and preparing to move out, but now how much you longed for those days you two were together.

You went down the long, stone stairway to the dormitory door, and gave the room key to the first educated youth you met. You told him that you might go away somewhere, and the key was for Dongzi, who was still at the hospital. The educated youth looked at you with surprised eyes, perhaps because you didn't carry anything with you, but he didn't ask you any questions for they all knew that usually your words were quite reserved. You went down the long road in the fac-tory area, passing those workers taking a walk and calmly answering their greetings, and you went to the two-storey building. The building looked very small in the twilight, and your guess was correct that all the lights on the first floor were out for they already got off work and left, while only the light in the director's office on the second floor was on. You were sure that only Wang Changhai was in the office at the time, and those who might come to play cards wouldn't come until half an hour later for they had to have supper at home first. The corridor was empty, the dome light was lit dimly, and the leaky faucet by the toilet made a dripping sound. The metal handle inside the building door felt cold, and an iron chain and lock were hung on it. After you went through the door, you locked it from inside and put its key into your pocket. You went up the empty stairs, your footsteps reverberating in the silence. You went to the room at the end of the corridor and, just as you expected, Wang Changhai was sitting at the desk alone.

Wang Changhai raised his head and your eyes met. A fluorescent lamp over his head gave a very strong bright light which cast his face under his eyebrows and nose in shadow. His face turned white but it seemed he didn't feel much surprise at your arrival, or to be exact, at the moment when he saw you he understood the situation at once. You took out the dagger from your sleeve and stabbed it into the desk as fast as possible.

You said, "We two should make things clear. If you are a real man, you can find something to fight with, otherwise don't blame me for being tough." You could feel your teeth chattering.

Wang Changhai raised his eyes from the dagger on the desk to look at you and smiled with a little surprise. He said slowly, "No, I will not run wild with you. When Dongzi did that detestable thing before, I didn't lose my mind, so today I advise you not to lose your mind either."

You were at a loss because you didn't expect him to be so calm.

He continued, "At that time, just based on the woman's accusation, if I, being the factory director, was serious, it was quite reasonable for me to get him caught and put behind bars for a few days even if he wouldn't have to be put into prison. But I didn't. Do you know the reason? Because I was not stupid and I knew it wasn't good for anybody if that matter turned serious. Today is the same situation. You must think I plotted the accident to break your brother's leg, but I can swear to God that it wasn't me who did it. Of course I know who did it, otherwise how can I deserve being the director? And indeed I really objected to it. You should have realized who they originally plotted the accident against and who they hate most."

"I know, it's me."

"Yes, it's you. Everybody at the factory knows it's you that the woman likes. Don't stop me and let me finish my words. It's you, but you yourself didn't want to get involved in the matter, which, to be honest, is what I appreciate in you. But though you kept on saying that you were not interested in her at all, why did you give your clothes to her to wear? Do you know how many persons the woman annoyed with your clothes? I am certain you should trust my analysis and judgment. So to resolve the matter, I wouldn't use that stupid method, and I have my own way, which is much smarter than that."

He took out two forms from a drawer, two forms for further study.

"These are two quotas for further study about cement manufacturing at Beijing Construction and Engineering Institute for a period of two years. I am now giving them to you two. Two years is not a short period, and I am sure you can find the way to go back to Beijing within the two years. So let's go our separate ways and not interfere with each other."

You pushed the forms away, and sneered, "But Dongzi's leg is broken! With these two helpless papers, can that be regained?"

"Yes," he said definitely, and pushed the forms to you again firmly. "Though broken, it can be set again. I have talked with the hospital and they confirmed it could be set. If not so, you can square the whole account with me then. Is that OK?"

You didn't speak. You took the two forms, but you abruptly stopped before you left and went back to the man who had been looking at you all the time.

"Your kindness is accepted, but blood demands blood." With these words, you cut two times on the arm of this white-faced man with your dagger. Then blood slowly oozed through his sleeve, which appeared to be a big red cross.

Two days later, you took Dongzi back to Beijing. When you were at the Institute for further study, the system of college entrance examination was restored. You passed the examination while Dongzi went to a forest in the northwest area. He chose to stay in the Northwest Plateau instead of trying to stay in Beijing with other educated youths.

Feng Ba

Actually, Feng Ba's name was not Feng Ba. Feng Ba was short for "Feng Bastard," or to be more accurate, "the bastard whose surname was Feng" for short, and this was the nickname Dongzi gave to his stepfather, from which you can see easily that Dongzi neither liked his stepfather nor respected him.

The actual Feng Ba in real life didn't look as ugly as his name, and instead he was a very tidy, timid, and even a little shy man. At one Chinese New Year when you went home to join your family, you went to Dongzi's home at his invitation. In that beautifully decorated dining room, you saw a well-dressed, handsome man with gray hair walking out of it, surrounded by several of his students. They called him Professor Feng or Mr. Feng. Professor Feng or Mr. Feng's face was very white, and so were his hands, and so was his shirt collar, all of which were quite different from Dongzi. He looked at you with some astonishment, and when you mentioned Dongzi's name, he nodded and said politely that he was here. His tone confirmed that he was the host of the house, instead of a guest as your first thought, or, in other words, he was Feng Ba.

At that small factory thousands of miles away from here, in the Northwest Plateau, in those long and boring afternoons, you once ate up the enemy of Dongzi after his being fried many times. In his narrative and your imagination, the man would be a rascal full of the smell of alcohol, walking fiercely in a dirty *hutong*, wearing a pair of plastic slippers of low quality bought on sale; his heels dirty, his yellowing vest stained with soy sauce. You didn't expect at all that he turned out to be a professor, a man who surprised you from his appearance to his manner.

Hearing our talking, Dongzi and his mother stuck their heads out from the kitchen. His mother looked quite old, and except for looking very tender, her sloppy and plain dress and her wide shoulders confirmed her blood relationship with Dongzi. In this house which seemed too big—except for the dining room, other rooms looked empty because of little furniture—Dongzi and his mother looked like two servants. They were like two grass baskets covered with mud misplaced by accident in this luxurious and scholarly house, and in this case the best place to hide them was the kitchen. And the situation that day proved this exactly.

Dongzi pulled you into the kitchen as soon as he stuck his head out from there. The kitchen was very dirty, and the ground was full of onion peels, vegetable leaves, and even fish scales. Dongzi, whose hands were full of scales, was helping his mother cook. At first sight you could perceive that Dongzi's mother came from a background neither wealthy nor hygienic. Her apron was stained with oil; her fingers were covered with flour; and on the chopping board, the dirty, unwashed vegetables full of mud were put together with the clean, washed ones. Dongzi did away with all formalities with you, and he just let you stand in the kitchen all the time. Even the dinner took place in the kitchen on a small, low table. (It could be surmised that Dongzi and his mother always had their meals on that table.) When you said that you wanted to have a look at the other rooms, Dongzi said with disdain, "It's just a measly house. What's the good of looking at it?"

Dongzi was kind-hearted by nature, so why did he disdain his intellectual stepfather so much? And how did Dongzi and his mother enter into this intellectual family? Or from another angle, how could Professor Feng Ba and Dongzi's mother, who was from a worker-peasant origin, meet and get married? His mother had been a worker in a textile factory and then she was a care worker in a hospital. These were really very interesting questions. But unfortunately, Dongzi didn't want to talk about these, and he just told me that his own father was an electrician in that textile factory his mother worked at and died of an accident. Speaking of Feng Ba, he always simply commented, "It's the bastard's luck to meet my mother!"

You knew his stepfather's name in the end, and attended his lecture. But that happened after Dongzi died, when you had already finished your postgraduate courses. From a poster on the campus, you got the news that "a famous university professor and also an academic leader of national key disciplines" would come to give a lecture, but only when you saw that handsome face, the clean shirt, as well as the quite white hands (because of too much washing) you recognized that he was Dongzi's stepfather. His research focused on a very rare field, and that day's lecture was about the relationship between the names of two very small officials in the *Old Book of the Tang Dynasty* and the *New Book of the Tang Dynasty*. Dongzi's stepfather did painstaking research on it for around twenty years and finally proved that the well-accepted concept was wrong, that the two names referred to the same office position administrating local finance and the different historical records were just a slip of a pen. Such a concept had been accepted by many scholars, including the most well-known experts in the history of the Tang Dynasty. You had to admit that Dongzi's stepfather had a very solid academic foundation and a very devoted attitude to his study. He was willing to spend as long as twenty years just to study the difference between two minor official names, which was definitely beyond the ordinary scholars' concentration. However, on the other hand, you also have to admit that such a kind of devotion brought about some loneliness at the top: during that lecture, the number of audience members who left midway proved this. In that auditorium which could hold more than a hundred persons, fewer than twenty stayed until the end of the lecture, among whom one was the host. Several persons were from the student union. Besides that, there were a couple of professors, some auditorium staff, as well as a few of his students. You were the only audience in the true sense, but the reason for you to stay was for Dongzi, instead of for any interest in the lecture itself.

During that period when Dongzi entered and left the mental hospital again and again, you once went to visit him. After he came back to Beijing he had no place to stay but that big, empty, and desolate house. A few years passed, and you found that his mother had a couple of fractures that caused her to walk unsteadily and, as a result, the rooms became even dirtier and sloppier. It seemed that as time went on the house followed more and more with Dongzi and his mother's style, until finally it became a complete warehouse. The professor, Dongzi's stepfather, became an outsider just temporarily living there. The situation was really like this: the professor stayed in his own study all day behind a closed door, and only Dongzi's mother could enter it. At lunchtime, you saw the old woman carefully push the door to go inside, carrying a tray of food, and she closed the door again carefully; or you saw her come from the room with the leftovers and close the door quietly. Now Dongzi could walk around the different rooms recklessly with a mocking smile. And you also found that besides a single bed put up temporarily in Dongzi's room, there was another single bed in another small room, which absolutely couldn't accommodate two adults. This confirmed your guess that Dongzi's mother was indeed a servant instead of a hostess in the house.

But were you so sure? In the professor's always closed and mysterious bedroom, wasn't it possible that there was a double bed? You admitted that such a curiosity was a little bit vulgar.

After that academic lecture with only a handful of listeners, Professor Feng stepped down from the platform and his students and the host hurried to go forward to support him while a couple of listeners ritually asked for his signature. You still sat in your seat, staring at him from a distance. You weren't certain that he saw you, or noticed you, or remembered you. At your limited visits to his home, the professor never came out from his study, so both you and he were quite strange and indifferent to each other. So you found,

shockingly, that he had undergone almost no change compared with the first time you met him. He was still handsome
and well-mannered, and even when facing such an awkward
situation or cold reception, he still kept his presence of mind.
You carefully checked his well-preserved face, in which you
couldn't detect any signs of aging, in order to see some mark
brought about by Dongzi's suicide. But you were disappointed, for the professor was undoubtedly above all worldly
troubles or humble emotions, flying on the magic carpet of
his own academic research. You heard the host apologize for
listeners leaving midway, and further talk about the current
impatient attitudes and money worship in academic circles,
and then you heard Professor Feng reply very mildly and
calmly with his southern accent, "The purpose of my study
is never for listeners."

You immediately felt awestruck at his words. You never
saw the professor talk with Dongzi's mother. During your
limited visits to their home, what you saw was always a static
and separated life—either the professor stayed in his study
or Dongzi or his mother stayed in the kitchen. There was a
middle area between the study and the kitchen which was
cold, silent, and carefully protected. This area was full of invisible wild grass and mesh wire, like a military demarca-
tion line. Whether you believe it or not, there wasn't a table
family members could sit around to have meals and talk at
all in such an empty house with several big rooms. You remembered that Dongzi once told you that he didn't have the
feeling of being at home in this house. You came back to Beijing very late because you went to college in another city and
had family here; Dongzi chose to stay in the northwest on
purpose. He said that he liked the forest and all the trees no
matter whether they were tall or low, strong or small, and he
felt very safe there. Dongzi did want to have a family in the
remote Loess Plateau, but in the end he had to leave—first
leave the girl, and then leave those trees.

In all fairness, Professor Feng did his duty as a stepfather
to Dongzi. After he left the cement factory, Dongzi went to
work in a local forest for a few years. Though he liked that

work very much, his mother worried about him all the time. Later the professor transferred him back to Beijing with his relations. It was quite reasonable for a highly respected professor to have a few capable students who, in turn, were willing to repay their teacher with their influence. Dongzi got a job at a research institute to distribute newspapers and administer stationery and envelopes. You didn't think Dongzi liked the job, but in others' eyes, this job seemed much better than farming or planting in the Loess Plateau, but Dongzi didn't show any gratitude to his stepfather and, on the contrary, his hatred for his stepfather seemed greater because of the job. In a depressed mood, he got married to a nurse and soon after that he was diagnosed with hepatitis. His depression further deteriorated because of his illness, and brought him from bad to worse in his relationships, and finally led him to quit, divorce, and even leave the world.

You once went to Dongzi's unit shortly after he got married. You got off the train and went straight to meet him. You found his office in a Russian-style brick building built in the beginning of the 1950s. All the offices were upstairs, while only his office was downstairs in the basement. The corridor of the basement was piled with debris and abandoned cabinets, and you had to pass through the chaotic mess to get to his room, which was a very small space emitting a moldy smell. Its high window was covered by rusty railings, and the grey sky light (not the sunshine) full of dust passed through these railings. The fluorescent lamp on the ceiling covered with water stains was on all day to shine down on those newspapers to be distributed, as well as the stationery and equipment. Every day Dongzi had one chance to get out of the basement, carrying the assorted newspapers and letters, to go to those bright rooms upstairs. He knocked on each office door, gave the newspapers and letters to the occupants, and asked one person in each office to sign a notebook. This was the only contact between Dongzi and those in the brightness. Dongzi told you that he had no reason to go upstairs except this. Of course, there was another exception:

when some person came downstairs to ask him to help move desks or to get some stationery.

In theory, he could go upstairs and go into those bright rooms to talk and communicate with others, but he didn't do so for whatever reasons. Perhaps this had something to do with his professor stepfather. Dongzi looked somewhat isolated and he seemed to have no intention to change it. It could be imagined easily that such isolation would become more serious after he got hepatitis. You felt uneasy because the dark basement surrounded by railings reminded you of prison or jail, which surely you didn't tell him. You said something that everybody else would say, such as that this was just the first step of a long march; that anyhow, it was a good thing to be back in Beijing; and that where there was life, there was hope, and so on and so forth. Dongzi sat at the window and listened to your clichés with a mocking smile, and finally he said something that left in you a deep impression. He said, "Don't you think that here is even worse than the 'cinder cave,' where there were a lot of prisoners, while I am alone here?"

After Dongzi died, it was at the end of that lecture that you had the first time, also the only time, to talk about Dongzi's situation with Professor Feng. You asked him why they sent Dongzi to the mental hospital in so short a time instead of letting him stay at home for treatment. The professor countered with the question whether you thought two elderly persons had the capabilities and strength to take care of such a sick person. Then you asked him whether he thought about changing a job for Dongzi, and he answered that was too difficult. He said that with his educational background it was already good enough to get that errand at the research institute. You noticed that the professor used "errand" instead of "job." You kept silent for a while, and then continued to ask him whether he had been to Dongzi's office, and he told you he had never been there and he also didn't think it was necessary, which undoubtedly somewhat irritated you, so you mentioned the gloom, the moldy smell, the loneliness, and

Dongzi's comparison with the "cinder cave." Your blame was obvious and you thought he would feel annoyed for Dongzi's ungratefulness, but on the contrary, he looked very calm and said slowly in his usual mild tone, "That's his own business. One of my graduate students was also from the basement."

You had no more words to say. You thought Dongzi himself had no more words to say because he had no ability to go to the second floor, or the third floor, or the fourth floor though being a graduate.

A necessary supplement to the ending

Many years later when you had a business trip to the north of Shannxi, you went to visit that cement factory in the mountain by the way. The previous narrow road for donkey passing became a very wide and bustling one. At a dumpling restaurant at the roadside, you and retired factory director Wang Changhai drank a whole case of beer. You talked about the experience of "guiding work" at Sujiagou, and those memorable persons and things at the factory. The passing of time eliminated all those grudges and rifts between you and him, and both of you became very composed, like two stones with polished edges and corners laying under water. You two sighed with emotion, patting each other's shoulder like brothers. Wang Changhai's hair had turned white and he looked quite old, but his big eyes, with wrinkles around them, were still very sharp. When he saw a beautiful woman, his eyes immediately started shining as before. He told you that all those educated youths had left except one or two who were too old to move anymore. He also told you that Shuizhen married a workshop director at the factory, who happened to be promoted to become factory director. Both of you smiled knowingly when he talked about this. But then Wang Changhai said scornfully, "Today's director can't be compared with the ones in the past at all, because now the factory belongs to us only in name, and indeed at least half of its property was sold to a Taiwan businessman, so the director is just a puppet." But he also admitted that Shuizhen's husband was very smart, for though the factory didn't get rich, his own family got rich. They even had two sets of duplex houses downtown, the kind of house having stairs inside. Very naturally, you asked about the situation of Shuizhen, and he laughed, "She got fat and doesn't work anymore. She is a housewife now, and has two sons. She wears two gold rings on her fingers!" You imagined the fat Shuizhen wearing gold rings and couldn't help laughing.

Wang Changhai said with self-deprecation and a faint tone of loss, "Women are really very strange animals, for if you think they have no brains, their eyes are very insightful. For instance, could you imagine what she would become today after she was pushed into the cesspit that year? Therefore, I always say women are just like cats that have nine lives, and will not die easily."

You turned the topic to his own wife and asked how she was, and he said that the poor woman died one year before. He bought a cemetery plot for her at the mount behind the factory, which was for both of them. He said that he would lie inside when his time was up. The tombstone was also ready for both of them, and as to the exact date—his was missing now. Then he laughed loudly. You laughed also, with some respect.

Of course, you talked about Dongzi. Wang Changhai sighed, "He was a good boy. He was sincere to others, but unfortunately his whole life went into a dead end, not like Shuizhen, who could fall into something but could also come out. He couldn't get out of it once he got caught." Wang Changhai looked at you with his radiant eyes, and said, "Hey, guy, I want to say something direct. On this matter, do you agree that you behaved not as well as Dongzi, nor as well as Shuizhen? But some persons are doomed to have a good life, and this is fate."

You didn't reply.

Wang Changhai narrowed his eyes mockingly, and asked you whether you wanted to see something. He rolled up his sleeve and then the blood-red cross scar appeared, which was raised a little on his skin and looked like a half-buried red earthworm. "You were quite cruel at that time, but do you know how I treated you? Actually, I was definitely able to beat you to death then because at that moment a few people were hidden in my office. I am telling you the truth that there were a few in my office at that time, for I knew you wouldn't let it go at that, and all of you educated youths were trouble-makers. So before you came to my office with the dagger, I had already hidden several persons in my back room in advance."

You were completely dumbfounded.

You should remember that hospital. That day, the third day after you talked with Wang Changhai, you checked both your luggage and Dongzi's, and, carrying those two admission recommendation forms, went to see Dongzi at the county hospital several dozens of li away. Unexpectedly, you met Shuizhen at the ward, who had come with two other women workers. She brought Dongzi a basket of red jujubes, which were said to nourish the blood. Dongzi couldn't walk because of a cast on his leg, so he talked with the others from his bed. He blushed from excitement and obviously seemed not to know how to handle the situation. Your arrival made him feel very happy, and he asked you to treat them. Shuizhen said that it was not necessary and they just came to say goodbye to both of you and would leave soon. You immediately realized that she already got the news from Wang Changhai that you would go back to Beijing for school.

When you saw them off, the other two women workers went away tactfully. You walked with Shuizhen to pass through the long corridor and come to the outside in the open. It was the beginning of the summer. An old acacia tree was blossoming with full, pink flowers with bees flying around them, and there was a very heavy fragrance in the air. You stopped at a big tree, the tree casting a shadow on your bodies.

You said, "We are going to school in a few days."

"I know," she said, gloom flashing across her face. Then there was silence, except for the hum of bees. "That's the reason for my coming—uh, no, I came for his leg." She hurried to correct her words. "I didn't expect things to turn out like this. I heard it from the director. I heard you went to him… Anyhow, I just want to say that you are really good persons. Perhaps, perhaps, it shouldn't happen, and I am sorry—"

You didn't expect she would speak like this, and you felt your heart beating a little faster. You interrupted her, "It's us who should apologize, especially me."

She raised her eyes to look at you, her face pale, and you even saw some tears in her eyes. She cast her dark eyes down, and she turned around at this moment. She ran out of the hospital gate quickly, wiping her eyes, while you stood there watching the little figure disappear in the trees' shadows outside the gate.

Dongzi

The city where you went to college was quite far from Beijing, but much nearer compared with the distance between the cement factory in the northwest of Shannxi and Beijing. Dongzi once passed this city when he went back to Beijing to see his family from his forest in the northwest, and he got off midway to see you. The Dongzi working at the forest was even darker than before, and he looked like a black iron tower on the campus. You took him to see your girlfriend, who was your classmate at that time and became your wife later. Dongzi stared at the young girl for quite a long time, smiling with a little gloom. That night you asked him for his comment on the girl, and he said, "Now I know what kind of girl you like."

You asked him what that kind was. Dongzi said that you liked the girls who looked like village girls. You felt puzzled, for your girlfriend was actually born in a city and she was a painter's daughter. But Dongzi was sure about his comment, and he said, "I know she isn't from a village, but I think her look is like a village girl." He pointed to the center of his own forehead. "Look here. Her forehead looks like a village girl's."

You two talked the whole night. Dongzi told you that he was in a dilemma of either keeping on at the forest or going back to Beijing. And he said that in order to persuade him to go back to Beijing, his mother even tried to find a girlfriend for him, who had graduated from nursing school and was an intern at a hospital in Beijing now. She was said to be quite pretty, and this time he came back to Beijing to meet her. But he said that he was not interested in the matter and he would rather stay at the forest than go back to a home devoid of human kindness. He said that his real interest was to stay in the forest to be with those trees, which were good to human beings and never schemed against us. He said seriously, "When you are in anguish, they can talk with you. This is true."

One year later, Dongzi wrote to you and told you that he got married to the nurse and would move back to Beijing.

Quite often you remembered Dongzi's comment about your girlfriend after judging her from her forehead. You remembered the first time you met her. You entered the classroom and saw her among a group of girls singing. She wore a faded shirt made of coarse cloth, which was dyed with blue pigment. She was smiling, with her two black braids over her shoulder, one in the front, and the other behind. You didn't know the exact reason but you were immediately touched by her smile. Now you know that it was because you had seen the smile before, when you were at the cement factory, which was a kind of shy, lonely, and a little sad smile, just like the flowers that opened in the cold wind though they might miss the proper season for blossom, and there was both some expectation and some disappointment in her smile. You had to admit they did have some resemblance. But you didn't tell Dongzi that your wife, though she came from the city and her parents were urban citizens, was sent to the countryside at a very early age and was brought up there.

You later went to Dongzi's bridal chamber in Beijing and you were shocked by its mess, dimness, and dirt. There wasn't any newly-married happiness in the house. The big red paper of happiness had almost lost its original color, but it was still attached to the window carelessly. Piles of newspapers, candies, and ashtrays were strewn across the table at random, while the stove covered with dust proved they hadn't cooked for quite a long time. And the most shocking thing was that there wasn't any photo of the newly married couple on the wall, but instead there was a small frame with the photo of you and Dongzi inside it. In the picture you two stood at the broad bank of the Yan River. Both of you were very young, wearing the grass-green uniforms, and while you were just smiling, Dongzi laughed heartily. His trouser legs were rolled up, and at his hand was his beloved fishing rod with a very long line. But now his face was grey-colored, and his look was listless, with a lit cigarette between his smoked-yellow fingers. He had become a totally different person from that energetic young man in the photo.

The pretty nurse appeared for a second when you arrived, and then left. She said that she had to visit a friend. Dongzi looked embarrassed at hearing this and in a somewhat blunt tone asked her to be back early. The nurse said goodbye to you politely, as if she didn't hear Dongzi's words at all. Her smiling gaze lingered on your face for a long time, and it seemed that she wanted to compare you with the person in the photo, which made you feel a kind of familiar but remote uneasiness. Her back looked like another face—some women did have this kind of capability that their backs were their other faces, which were charming and flirtatious.

Your guess was confirmed by Dongzi later. That deep night when both of you were utterly drunk, Dongzi told you everything. He told you that the woman was a bitch, a bitch from the countryside. She had men as early as when she was in the village. His eyes turned red, and he said that one of the men who dumped her after violating her was an educated youth from Beijing.

Dongzi told you that when he met the woman for the first time, he did have a crush on her although he always kept saying that he liked only trees instead of women, which was a complete lie for a man at his age. He just didn't feel self-confident about himself. Unexpectedly, when they met, the nurse looked very enthusiastic. He found that she was pretty, lovely, and clever, and she wasn't disgusted with his appearance nor the fact that he was only a worker working in another city. Dongzi was truly overjoyed. However, very soon he found out the truth, that it was not he who she was interested in, but his stepfather, a professor of the university, because at that time she wanted to stay in Beijing and the clinic of the university was, of course, the best choice. But Dongzi tolerated all this, considering he himself really had nothing special. Their relationship developed quickly and was confirmed after they met only one or two times. Afterward, Dongzi went back to the forest and they kept writing very short courtesy letters with each other until they finally got married.

Dongzi told you, "On our wedding night, I knew the whole story. She was quite straight and told me everything. She said 'You couldn't expect me to be a virgin.' She said when she was still a little girl, she already played that kind of game with boys in the village. When she grew older, she met an educated youth from Beijing and fell in love with him. She even aborted for him, but later the educated youth dumped her and went back to Beijing. She told me her purpose in getting married to me was nothing but to stay in Beijing, and then if someday she met that guy on the street, she wanted him to know she could come to Beijing without him. You should know who her words made me remember, and you should also know my feeling. You know, right? And only you know. I asked myself in my heart whether this was fate. Perhaps it was. I told myself that I shouldn't care about the matter, for I once did something evil, and now I had to take the consequences. I would treat her well. Maybe we couldn't become the best couple, but at least we could make do with life. However, it didn't work. I tried, but I failed. Before her, I couldn't be a man anymore. I couldn't make myself be a man, never ever. Don't you think this was fate?" Dongzi laughed loudly. That night, just like at the cement factory many years ago, you hugged him on the shoulder tightly.

After that meeting, there was a period as long as eight years during which you got married to your girlfriend; had your own family in a remote city far from Beijing; had a daughter; moved from one unit to another; and finally through examinations became a graduate student in Beijing, which was the only way for you to come back to Beijing. During the eight years, you and Dongzi had a few brief communications. He complained to you about those persons and things of his unit, and you advised him to be tolerant to them. Neither of you mentioned your respective marriages until one day he told you that he got divorced. It was the nurse who asked for it, and her reason was that Dongzi had hepatitis and he was ill-tempered. You wrote to him to comfort him, but didn't get his reply.

One year you had a business trip to another city, and when you came home your wife told you Dongzi had visited. Your wife said that she saw a dark and thin man standing at the door when she arrived home after work. He was carrying a travel bag, and looked fatigued from travelling. Your wife said that she immediately realized he must be Dongzi, but he wasn't anymore that young man like an iron tower from many years before. He had changed a lot and became a man of few words. When he looked at your wife, it seemed he didn't know her. Your wife asked him to come into the house and she prepared to make some tea for him, but he stopped her and said he had hepatitis. This surprised your wife, but she was a kind woman so she hurried to say that didn't matter and insisted on him having some tea, while Dongzi also insisted his refusal. He kept asking where you went, and your wife told him that you went to some place in the south for a business trip. Then he asked the exact place you went, and after your wife told him you went to Nanjing, he became silent. Your wife took fruits and seeds to him, but he didn't react. He kept silent and for more than one hour he just sat there without any words, and then abruptly he asked your wife whether there were some photos of you. He wanted to see your photos. Your wife felt weird at this request, but she took out the photo albums of your family anyway. There were many photos of your wife and daughter in the albums, such as photos of your daughter at different ages, and the photos of your wife holding your daughter playing on a tour, all of which were taken by you, so you seldom appeared in the photos except several ones with your wife and daughter or a few group photos with some irrelevant strangers because of having meetings together. It was a very small number in total, because you didn't like photography.

Your wife pointed you out in the photos to him and told him that you became fat and grew a beard. Dongzi told her that she didn't need to point for him, because he knew your appearance. He looked at these photos for quite a long time. First he tried to find your vague figure in those crowds, and then his gaze stayed on your face with a look of loneliness and a smile of thoughtfulness. Your wife said that she had never seen a man stare at another man in such a focused way. Then he returned these photos to your wife, stood up, and left with his travel bag and he didn't tell your wife where he might go. You wrote to him at your wife's urging, but the letter was returned with the words "No such person" on its envelope.

Finally, you and your wife went back to Beijing through the examinations. And during the first year in Beijing there were certainly a lot of things to do, such as moving house, settling down, having classes, and preparing for tests, so you didn't remember to contact Dongzi until one year later, which was the end of a full year. You got the phone number of his stepfather's home from a pile of old notebooks, tried dialing it, and got through easily. The voice from the other end of the phone was old and cold, but you immediately recognized his stepfather's sound. When you asked to talk to

Dongzi, he kept silent for a while and then guardedly asked who you were. You told him your name and that you were Dongzi's friend, and then he told you that Dongzi was already at the mental hospital.

You didn't expect that after a separation of eight years it would be at a mental hospital that you met Dongzi again. The hospital, Anding Hospital, was a very famous mental hospital. Your heart twitched when you saw Dongzi walking toward you from a crowd of sluggish-looking patients wearing hospital gowns. He looked much older. The muscles on his face had become slack, and his face looked very fat because of his short-cut hair. His glassy eyes made him no different from other patients. But when he saw it was you who was standing in the corridor, his eyes became shining for a moment, which meant he recognized you and he remembered you. His look at you was the only cogent look. Later, when you both sat down at a table and started talking, gradually you found that he was no longer the Dongzi from before, and the Dongzi here and now had gone into a world beyond your reach. You were separated from him by a wall, a glass wall that you couldn't see and you couldn't go through either. But since he went behind the wall, he was also into a state of indestructible isolation as cold as ice.

Anyhow, Dongzi liked to see you and he was looking forward to it. His mother told you that when it was time for your visit, he would become restless. In the early morning he put on his clothing neatly, waiting for you at the window, and he would ask the nurse or his family members again and again whether it was time for a visit or why you didn't come yet. And every time when you were leaving, he was always standing against the wall, just as a punished student would stand. He stood there timidly with his hands at his sides, lowering his head to look somewhere on the ground. You asked him to go back to his ward, but he asked you to go first, still looking at the ground instead of you when he muttered the words. He didn't ask when you would come to see him next time, but you knew he wanted to ask so you told him that you would come to see him during the holiday. He nodded seriously, his eyes still looking at the ground, until you left, far from him, and had even already disappeared from the long corridor. Only then did he go slowly back to his ward.

Every year you went to see Dongzi twice: once at the mid-autumn festival and again at the lunar New Year's Eve, as you had promised. But one lunar New Year's Eve you didn't go, and the following mid-autumn you didn't go either. After that, Dongzi committed suicide.

As to the reason why Dongzi stored so much toilet paper, his mother had her own explanation. She told you that indeed he had thought of different ways to ask us to see him, while on the other hand, during his last days, even she was afraid to see him, because every time he could sit calmly with you only for the first minute, then things changed. For instance, one day when Dongzi was talking with his mother, he stopped suddenly and looked severely at someone across from him. He said, "You go away," which shocked his mother because at that moment they were talking about the sour cabbage that was Dongzi's favorite in his early years. At first, his mother thought she had got it wrong, so she asked him what he said. Dongzi answered, "You go away." When his mother prepared to stand up, Dongzi told her to sit there for he was not speaking to her. Then he pointed seriously to somewhere behind his mother and said, "Didn't you hear my words? What we are talking about has nothing to do with you, so leave at once!"

Frightened, Dongzi's mother turned back to look, but there was nobody.

Dongzi shouted angrily at an invisible person, or maybe a group, "Don't try to deceive me! Don't think I don't know you are a group! You can't come here! Don't be furtive in the corner, or whisper to each other, or make trouble out of nothing, or spread slanderous rumors, or arouse hatred among others! Do you want to blind me by dazzling my eyes with the mirror facing the sun? Or do you want to deafen me by clanging the iron pipe downstairs or cutting the floor with an axe? You drive a car on my heels and want to kill my shadow, and you even follow my mother because you think she is old and there is a hole in her skirt through which you can see Tiananmen Square—is that right? You think others don't know what you are doing, and you can do these things secretly. No! No! No! You are wrong! Totally wrong! The guilty can never escape Heaven's justice! There is the sun in the sky; there is the moon on the ground; there is the dragon king in the sea; there are policemen on the street; and there are persons everywhere. As long as there is a person, there are eyes, so there are eyes everywhere: sun's eyes, moon's eyes, persons' eyes, animals' eyes, trees' eyes. These eyes can walk, fly, and fire bullets! The east wind is blowing; we are beating the drum. In today's world, who is more afraid in the end?!"

Dongzi started to sing in a sort of growl, slapping on the table, and then the doctors came to get involved. Well, you know, the doctors there were quite different from the doctors in the usual sense—they were just some husky nurses and their job was to prevent patients from launching into this kind of weird reasoning or experiencing extreme emotional catharsis. But they couldn't hold back his mother's tears. His mother was crying.

Before this event, you once tried to make Dongzi realize that his ideas were wrong. You told him that it was wrong to say there was the sun in the sky and there was the moon on the ground because both the sun and the moon were in the sky.

Dongzi refuted you. "No, I see the moon on the ground. It is in the water."

Then you said, "The moon in the water is just the reflection of the moon in the sky, while the real moon is in the sky."

Dongzi asked you quietly, "Why isn't the real moon in the water while the moon in the sky is its reflection?"

You were speechless.

Usually when Dongzi was with you he didn't become manic easily, and, according to his explanation, it was because you two were so powerful that "they" didn't dare to come. You asked him, "When do they usually come here?"

He answered a little bit unwillingly, "That depends, because this is a very complicated question."

You continued to ask, "But how do you know?"

"Here." He pointed to the center of his head.

You tried to guess. "Use your head to think?"

He said mysteriously, "No, not to think, but to see."

You remembered that Dongzi once used the eye to "see" your wife.

Dongzi told you that when you were there, "they" would not dare to come. He said, "When you are here, they don't dare to bully me. Because you are the right hand, while I am the left hand, and the left hand and the right hand are together. There are two hands in total."

After Dongzi died, you accompanied his mother to the mental hospital to pack his things. There were bits and pieces of snowflakes not melted yet in the winter's open country, and the air was cold and chilly. In the car, Dongzi's aging mother told you how Dongzi went mad. It happened several years before, when he was still working at that research institute. Then one day, without any omen, he suddenly left the unit carrying a travel bag but not telling anyone else. He simply disappeared from the city for exactly ten days. At that time people thought he had an accident or got lost because no one knew where he had gone, except that they found a note on his table: "I am going to look for my hands."

She cried, and said, "You see? Was he mad at that time? He must have been mad at that time!"

You didn't answer her, but you remembered Dongzi's visit to your home. You were wondering why, one year or maybe two years before, you stopped seeing him when he was looking forward to your visit so helplessly. The first time was when you hurried to deliver a speech at an academic conference where many foreign specialists and well-known experts would get together, and so you thought that it was very important for your professional stature. You wrote the speech day and night and you didn't remember to see Dongzi until the conference was over and you read your paper, but you had already missed the date you had promised him. The second time was when you finally didn't get the professional title which should rightly belong to you and you were completely tired of that kind of infighting at the unit, so you left and went into business to be a department manager at a company. That afternoon, with the general manager, you were appointed to entertain a very important customer with enormous potential for new business. At a very well-known restaurant in Beijing, when you made the toast to congratulate the "successful cooperation" between the customer and your company, you heard the customer mention that it was the mid-autumn festival that day. His words stirred your heart because you remembered your appointment with Dongzi, but instead you immediately said the following words: "It can be clearly seen that this is our fate arranged by God, that we can be together here with our distinguished customer at such an unforgettable festival."

You felt ambivalent that night at the restaurant, and you did think of asking for permission from the general manager and going to see Dongzi for it was not too late then and the mental hospital and the restaurant happened to be in the same direction, so you might as well arrange such a visit. But at that moment, the general manager came and told you that for the sake of future business with the customer, it would be better for you to take him to another well-known resort to enjoy a happy night. As a result, you got into that brand new Buick, the nice and wide company Buick, and the customer, the general manager, and you rested on the soft cushions a little bit drunkenly. You were all in a good mood for you had a good dinner and talked about the business easily, so you were filled with a kind of warmth to life, to the world, to the future, and to all the people. The car drove steadily to the outskirts of the city. In the darkness, there appeared a light and a black building, and the customer asked what that was and you told him calmly that it was Anding Hospital, the most famous mental hospital in China.

Now you finally understand why Dongzi left you and committed suicide, and you also understand why, after he died, by some unseen power you lost the last chance to see him again at the funeral hall. All these were caused by that night, yes, that night, when you were with the customer at the resort. You went to bed very late that night after you escaped from the flashing neon lights, the rotation of music and dance, the transpiration of the fog of the sauna, as well as the deafening roar of bowling. You crawled back to the deluxe room, and you threw yourself down on the bed exhaustedly. You dropped off very soon and fell into dreaming.

You dreamed of going to see Dongzi finally, but not that night. It was the night many years before when you went to see newly-married Dongzi. In that empty bridal room, you and Dongzi cooked a meal just as you did at the cement factory in Northwest Plateau. Dongzi made your favorite fried fish, and you two talked as you drank. At last Dongzi was drunk, and he told you about what happened between him and the nurse. He said that he had nobody else to talk to because nobody except you had lived in his most intimate world. His original words were that you lived in his heart, instead of just living together at the dormitory. He said you were the right hand while he was the left hand, and the right hand and the left hand should be one person. He asked you to remember and to remember forever that his best time in life was with you. You were shocked by his words, for you didn't expect that he would express such feelings. You also talked about the dog, Baba, whom Dongzi said he often dreamed of these days, and he said that he dreamed you held it while walking in the snow. While in a trance, it seemed well; it even had a family and gave birth to a lot of baby dogs, but then the dream turned back to the snow where you and he still held Baba and walked forward together anxiously.

After this you remembered something, so you asked Dongzi whether he still remembered those stars, those feathered stars. He nodded his head in certainty and said that of course he remembered those big and feathered stars. You said that they were alive and could fly, and he agreed that they were alive and could fly. You asked whether you saw them on the way to the Qinghai-Tibet Plateau, and he said he forgot but mentioned it was at night and you and he saw them together. But you still had doubts about the location because you remembered you went to the Qinghai-Tibet Plateau by truck and didn't get off, which meant you had no chance to see the stars. Dongzi smiled at your reasoning and said, "Why couldn't you see the stars without getting off the truck? You could see as long as you wanted." Then you had another idea that perhaps it happened on the night when you held Baba; he agreed again that it happened on the night when you held Baba. You told him in that case Baba must have seen them also, and he immediately confirmed Baba must have seen them.

When you woke up, you found Dongzi was cooking breakfast. The boiled eggs were ready and put in a bowl for you. The eggshells had been carefully cracked, and the broken eggshells with the mottled color of soy sauce gave off a fragrant aroma. You knew Dongzi made these eggs for you specially because you liked eating eggs. You put on your clothes sleepily and wanted to pull open the curtain but Dongzi stopped you, and he asked you to see the ray, and the dim light, which looked just like the morning at the dormitory of the cement factory.

In the end, you must dream of that morning when Dongzi sent you to the station. Drizzle was floating in the air and the ground, wet by the rain, reflected an illusory light. You two walked side by side silently. At that time you didn't know that it was the last time you would walk with a sane Dongzi, and you didn't know that you were missing something that you missed before. You stepped on the gate, took the luggage Dongzi passed to you as well as that bag of eggs, and walked forward along the narrow compartment. Through the window you could see Dongzi's hairy head at the platform. He also walked following your direction, and he looked toward you as he was walking. You knew he tried to catch up with you and he hoped that you would stop somewhere to open the window and exchange some last words with him. He wanted to talk with you and he still had words to tell you. But you didn't stop, and you knew you were destined not to open the window or talk with him because you didn't find an empty seat yet for you to stop. So you still had a long way to go. The train would start in a minute, for the time was up, and the moment, the moment destined to leave him, was coming.

—May 3, 2004, the first manuscript
—May 7, 2004, the second manuscript
—December 20, 2004, the third manuscript

From "The Waste Land"

The creation of The Third Person

On a summer evening of a few years ago, whose exact date I can't remember, I sat at the window without turning on the light, reading *The Waste Land* by T.S. Eliot, which is a work that I like very much but always vaguely understand. In different situations or in different moods, my understanding of such a masterpiece that is not quite long but has an extremely vast content was sometimes clear while sometimes vague. Luckily, I was in a good state that day. And I read such a sentence: "Who is the third who walks always beside you?" Since I had clarity of mind at that time, I also carefully read the densely-printed remarks under it, in which the author wrote: "It was inspired by the experience of an Antarctic expedition group. It was said when those explorers were totally worn out, they would have such an illusion that they felt there was one more team member in the group every time when they checked the number." These words made me, who originally felt very hot all over, suddenly feel a burst of cold on my back for no reason, and the chill from the depths of my bones also startled my mind, so I hurried to take a piece of paper and wrote the three words: "the third person."

After writing the three words, this small piece of paper, together with many other notes, was put into my notebook. With many times of moving houses, its color gradually turned yellow to embody its experienced time. I have a lot of such papers on which there were only a few scribbled words or phrases from some hearsay. They might be about what happened in my dreams, or my reading thoughts, or just an inexplicable glimmering, and they were just like seeds forgotten in a corner, falling fast asleep, nourished and brewed by memories and imaginations subconsciously and inadvertently. Some of them would be lucky that maybe one day when I turned to the notebook at random, they might be singled out to be sown into the computer, budding, leafing out, flowering, and finally growing into a tree of a novel.

The Third Person is just such a tree to grow up slowly. For many years I knew I would write such a story, a story about a person's illusion in a desperate condition, but I didn't know what such a story wanted to express, just as to a bottle with a concrete shape at my hand, I didn't know what kind of water should be put into it. Until one day, when I finally found this theme and found the inner world of the characters, or, in other words, I finally knew who the "third person" was. This is a story about suffering and dreamland; or about sinking and transcendence. I developed two fleeing prisoners in a desert, who were at the brink of desperation but still desired to survive. They should have been desperate to take any action unscrupulously but they suffered from the torture and tracings of conscience. Because of conscience, the justifiability of trying to survive—which shouldn't be questioned—became a question for them, and in the end, due to the guilt for their companion, they gave up escape and struggle. The question that the novel posed was: Facing the plain struggle between life and death, is it possible for people to still keep their dignity and conscience? And can death be transcended? Does death have any actual meaning? And for those who committed sin and are doomed to die, can they purify themselves by sacrificing their physical bodies? At the end of the novel, the "I," being a juvenile offender, gave up the survival of his physical body in the world to gain the redemption of his soul from heaven, and the hand, which was stretched into the buried cave in the hour of death, was the hand of "the third person," and it was also the symbol of conscience and redemption.

From *Family History* to *The Third Person* there was a similar theme to be touched upon: suffering as well as a sense of guilt. If we say that suffering is the fate of humanity, those who experienced suffering but didn't feel guilty, or who failed to repent, are hopeless and their souls can't be redeemed. Even today I still can't forget Dostoevsky's quest for the same question in his work *The Brothers Karamazov*. The image of the priest's brother who was still full of grateful tears to God's grace, even facing death, deeply touched me. And I realized that a great work was surely beyond personal resentment and had great compassion and affection for mankind's suffering. In this sense religion is essential, while such a symbolic novel as *The Third Person* is perhaps also meaningful.

The above words suggest that we can often draw inspiration and ideas from great works; under the reflection of Russians' great religious spirit by Dostoevsky; and in the vast and abundant wilderness of Eliot, this novel, at best, is just one small tree with a little ingenuity derived from them.

—June 9, 2005 in Beijing (originally contained in No. 7, 2005 *Beijing Literature-Novel Monthly*)

To Kneel in Front
of Memory

The creation of My Left Hand

It's really out of my expectation that *Beijing Literature-Novel Monthly* reprinted three of my novels within one year, to which I feel both grateful and nervous.

The creation of *The Third Person* was the same as most of my novels, having experienced quite a long deliberation. Actually, some of its paragraphs were written many years ago, but over time I couldn't find the "core" to pull all the plots together. I am usually slow to respond, so what's happening at present may touch me, but can't bring me the immediate inspiration and passion for creation; that is to say, the story in my heart can't become a real novel until I take a long time for it to accumulate and for me to deliberate. And that is the reason why I have written "historical" novels.

Thirty years ago there was a cement factory near Yan'an, which was built in a mountain area, and at this factory there were a lot of educated youths from Beijing, as well as some locals who were transferred from different communes nearby. They themselves built the factory building and the dormitory, brick by brick. Many stories took place among them, and they spent their youth there. But later, most of the educated youths left there by way of college entrance examination, or retirement because of illness, or other legal or illegal ways, and the cement factory in the mountain became just a memory in their hearts. My husband was one of those Beijing-educated youths at that cement factory at the time, and Dongzi was one of his closest friends. Among the six educated youths working on the same production team with him, in as short as twenty years, one person died and two persons became insane. Dongzi died after becoming insane.

As with *Family History* and *The Third Person*, this novel indeed wants to express the same feeling: a bad conscience. It is the survivors' memorial and mourning to the unfortunate, and it is also the survivors' introspection and repentance to their own hearts. In the era without priests and repentance, we can only kneel in front of memory.

In life, people have to forget something or give up something in order to live on and have a better life. Then what should we forget, or give up, or abandon? This is not a fresh topic; instead, it's an obsolete and ancient one. But this obsolete and ancient topic is actually an eternal topic, because it confuses people still and it has no answer.

—September 10, 2005 in Beijing

Childhood

My Autobiography

I.

In my childhood I was an unsociable kid. To play with other, lively kids was an extravagant wish unattainable for me, let alone to have one or two inseparable good friends. Usually I went out alone, holding a bamboo stick, poking here or hitting there, and going as far as I could. I never greeted anybody, and I was used to getting lost, so whether I would arrive home safely was always my mother's worry. Only I knew where I would go—either the desolate ditch full of wild grasses behind the dining room, or the big fruit tree nursery in front of my father's office building, which was my secret garden. I remember one day when I stood in the grass as high as a tree for me, looking at the flaming red sunset in the west slowly sinking into the haze, with my eyes abruptly welling exciting tears. Such a feeling was truly premature for a five- or six-year-old kid. In the novel, the scene in which the sensitive Yunyun was shut outside the door, sobbing alone, was my childhood's truest portrayal. Loneliness was my earliest life experience and has been accompanying me all the time. So far I haven't learnt how to communicate with others effectively, although from outward appearances I look mild, kind, and easy-going.

In the novel *Story of Huangyangbao*, I wrote about a girl named Yunyun, who looks independent and uninhibited in appearance but who is sensitive and delicate at heart. One night she went someplace to listen to stories with her mates, but was shut outside the door by mistake. She wanted to knock on the door but was afraid of being refused. She wanted to go back alone but was afraid of the dark, and as a result, she just stood outside the door crying for a full two hours. I didn't realize the exact meaning of the story until many years later, and I wrote it in the novel:

> A girl was crying, standing outside a door. A girl stood outside a door in the darkness, crying. This was more a symbol than a scene. Each one of us comes to the world out of our mother's womb, but we have to go into life by ourselves in a certain way, and in this sense we all have to experience birth two times: in the first birth our physical body separated from the midst of chaos to go into life, while in the second birth our soul must experience another separation to go into the world. Those people in the primitive tribes achieved such a separation through the ceremony of becoming an adult; through some unique secret ceremony; through meditation; through isolation; or through very cruel practice; while Yunyun achieved it through darkness and facing that tightly-closed door. It was just through this way that she realized her own existence—the isolated and helpless self separated from the world—that she understood the relationship between herself and the world. For her, the world was just like the door towering in front of her. So from here we can understand the actual meaning of that dark cave for her: if the world is the door, that cave is her mother's womb. To a kid standing outside the door all the time, going back to the cave means to go back to the chaos before birth. So it is in this sense that we can say that no matter how many years she has lived and how much she will experience, mentally-speaking, she isn't born yet. Yes, Yunyun is just a not-born-yet kid.

The above paragraph is the portrayal of my inner experience.

II.

In my childhood, I liked eating books, and my method was this: I took a book, one hand holding the front cover, the other holding the back cover, as if holding the two wings of a roast chicken. I tore the book into two sides with the pages of the book spreading out like drooping feathers, and then I opened my mouth to bite the edge of the paper to tear it down. Before I was three, my most impressive feat was to eat up my father's whole big box of collected books. My father was a painter, so a large number of his collection were picture-story books, which today we call comic books. The thickness and texture of this kind of book was particularly suitable for my taste, so I ate up all of them. Of course, I didn't swallow all of them and most of the time I just bit them into pieces like a mouse. The consequence of such an action was that I learned to read very early. (Before I went to elementary school, I already finished reading *Song of Ou Yanghai*, a very thick book.) But without the teacher's help on pinyin, though I could understand the meaning of each sentence quickly, I couldn't read them out loud correctly. Sometimes the mistakes I made were horrible. For instance, for quite a long time I misread "sigh" to "angry again," or misread "depression" to "tear sadly." Besides, since I ate books so madly, when later I realized these books were for reading instead for eating and I wanted to read them, there were few books left in our home. At that time, our whole society was short of books, so I had to look everywhere for books to read. When I couldn't find books, I just looked for anything with words on it. Occasionally, I might find some booklets without beginnings and endings, the papers used for pasting on the wall, the shoe patterns cut by my mother, the old newspapers put at the bottom of the drawers, or some torn paper covering an old jar of salted vegetables. As long as there were words on them, I would carefully read them for a long time with great pleasure.

When I was in high school there was a girl in my class who was short and unimposing in appearance, with average scores, but she became a classmate whom I was most eager to make friends with because this girl with a nickname of "paper doll" could find a lot of banned books. Nobody knew where she got them, but according to my observation she herself didn't read them, and these books actually belonged to others. However, her most unexpected capability was that she could collect those books into her hands in ways I didn't know about and then she used them to turn over or exchange with others very efficiently, which made her become a very special and important student in our class. I longed to obtain books from her, but I was newly transferred to the class, and my lofty character and my slender purse didn't allow me to ask her for any of them. She must have realized this, and one day, as usual, she walked up and down the aisle between the seats, busy doing some business calmly, and then suddenly she stopped at my seat, speaking loudly. "I have the book *Struggles in an Ancient City*, which will be returned to me this Thursday." Instead of looking at me, her small eagle-like eyes with a hint of pride turned to another girl. That girl said that she had already read it but unfortunately its ending was missed. Then I ventured to say that I hadn't read it, and she gave me a quick glance and said that I could read it but asked with what other book I could exchange it. I told her I had the book *Song of Ou Yanghai*, but she said with scorn that one couldn't be counted, and then I told her in despair I had no more books. She thought for a while, passed me her math exercise book, and said, "OK, then you do the homework for me."

Her book of *Struggles in an Ancient City* actually didn't have the ending part, and it was the same case for her book *Family* and her book *How the Steel Was Tempered*, but I was still very grateful to her. She was the first person with commercial awareness whom I got to know, and I think nowadays she must have become quite rich.

I went to college in 1978, and in those glass cabinets at our college library I finally found the books that I was once so eager to read. I started to read them one after another following the sequence that they were put in the open shelves at the reading room, without much understanding, plan, or regularity. In order to read those books that were not easy to borrow at usual times, I even gave up going home during vacations. And even now I often dream that I am a young college student, walking to the newly-lit library at twilight. I know I will find the books I want to read but I worry that I won't find a vacant seat or those books have been taken by others.

Wanting to read; being afraid of no books to read; and thinking my reading is too little became my whole life's anxiety, and maybe because of a guilty conscience from eating up and destroying so many books in my childhood, I always read in a hurry, with tension and little learning. I have done a lot of reading notes and have written down countless paragraphs either with deep meanings or beautifully written, but I seldom spent time digesting or thinking over their thoughts. I admire those who can read a book many times and absorb everything of it into their own mind through their contemplation. Moreover, I have to agree that a person's memory is just like a bottle, and its volume is in inverse proportion to his age. After graduation those sprint-like reading sessions made my mind become a racecourse of numerous thinkers, and through much dazzle and uproar what was left was often the loss after the dust settled.

I became a book editor after graduation and started the work of making books. While knowing clearly a book's secrecy from its manuscript to its final draft, I lost the mysterious feeling for books, so I decided to write my own. From eating up books in my childhood to writing books myself, it seems I do have an affinity for books. However, I know very well that among the voluminous books at present, those that should actually be kept and passed into the treasure house of human thought are few and far between. A really good book is created by its author with his whole life's wisdom and effort, as well as the most sincere and most beautiful things in his life, which is just like the wine brewed by bone marrow whose weight is exactly the same as a heart's weight, no more and no less.

III.

When I was a little girl, I liked drawing pictures very much, so instead of a novel my first published work was a folio-sized New Year painting with a rural theme. I made the painting when I went to the countryside to live and work at sixteen years of age. The title of the painting was "Glory Belongs to the Teachers of People." This seemed quite natural for me because my father was a painter, and those adults who knew me expected me to be a painter in the future, but I knew what I liked to draw most were the movie posters with plots and characters. Usually I first made the story drafts in my mind (they came from the stories I improvised and told to my girl mates during the breaks between classes), and then drew the movie posters, accompanied by the names of writers, directors, and main actors and actresses, and with many pictures of their plots and text descriptions. I usually hid them in very secret places, but one day when I came home from school, I found my mother as well as my sisters sitting around the table. They looked at me, their faces wearing strange and knowing smiles, and then my mother declared, "Welcome home to the author of *Haitao* [the screenplay name of my invention]!"

Although I dreamed of making up stories at an early age, I didn't try writing and submitting for publication until I was about thirty-years-old. My first novel, published in 1988, had a very strong magical flavor. During that period I worked as an editor at a magazine of biographies of Party historical figures in Shannxi. *Going to the Future* was an influential theoretical publication of that time. Its emphasis was ideology, and my novel was the only literary work published in it. The magazine I worked at later stopped publication, and my own writing was set aside because of a change of work and life. It was in 1995 that I really started my literary creation in a strict sense. Due to a chance invitation from my classmate at college, Pengwei, I joined the writing of a set of ancient war documentary novels because my major at college was history. As a result, the around 300,000-word historical novel, *The Kunyang Blood Riding*, was published by People's Liberation Army Literature and Art Publishing House in 1996. The writing of this novel not only brought me a request for my next works, but also got me acquainted with Liu Jing, who was a female editor and writer with a generous and gallant heart, and it was she who encouraged me to become engaged in the writing of novels and stories, and offered me the chances to attend writers' conferences.

War Nursery Rhymes was published in *PLA Literature and Art* in 1997, and it was my first novel published in a literary magazine. Mr. Liu Liyun, a poet, and the managing editor of my works, not only gave me some advice and help on this rather "different" work from a military theme, but he also attached an effusive comment written by himself. After its publication it was reprinted by *Novel Monthly* and *Xinhua Digest*, and won the PLA Literary Award from 1997 to 1998. It was also incorporated in the *China Selected Short Fiction* of that year compiled by the creation and research department of the China Writers Association, and in another set of *Military Novel Volume of Literature in 1990s* published by Beijing Normal University Publishing House. From then on I started my cooperation with the publications *Shanghai Literature, Chinese Writers, Harvest, Yan River, Beijing Literature, People's Literature,* and *October*, and I published my novel collections, *War Nursery Rhymes* and *You Can't Understand My Dream*, as well as the novels *Story of Huangyangbao* and *Li Tomb*. Many of these works were reprinted and received mention by some critics, and among them the more influential ones were *The Son of Tribulus, Family History*, and *My Left Hand*.

From 1988 when I published my first novel until in 1997, *War Nursery Rhymes* caused social concern. I spent around ten years before returning to literature, and stepped into the door of literature at forty-years-old. Perhaps I started a little later, but I still feel very grateful to fate for getting me engaged in writing, to extend my dream started in childhood, and to bring some meaning to my unremarkable life.

At last, I want to talk a little about my understanding of novels. I think the novel is a kind of literary style suitable for me, for I am not a sociable person and I like to speak hidden behind those characters and plots of novels. As time passes, with more and more writing, I have gained some understanding about novels—following is an article published in *Literary Gazette*.

A Door and a Dream

My understanding of novels

I.

One day in September 2002, the eyes of the whole world were concentrated on an ancient tomb on the banks of the Nile River, because on that day Egyptian archaeologists used a small robot to go through the thick stone wall and enter into the queen's grave at the Pharaoh Khufu tomb to disclose to the whole world a secret hidden for 6,000 years. The archaeologists had prepared for two years for this moment, and more than a hundred TV stations around the world broadcast the program. The anchors, scholars, and archaeologists gathered together to guess what was in the grave, using their knowledge and imagination. A pile of rare treasures luckily escaped from the ghouls? A mummified body of a woman with a mysterious smile covered by several thousand years' dust? A papyrus map drawn with the astrology and geography in Egyptians' eyes 6,000 years ago? But when finally the robot turned its front light, which was also a human being's curious eye, to the darkness kept silent for 6,000 years, all the people were speechless—there was a door! Except for a door, there was nothing else.

I inexplicably felt this was a novel. A good novel just vividly tells us like this how archaeologists imagined and guessed cheerfully; how they experienced difficulties and hardships; how they hopefully explored; but it also tells us there was nothing except a door at the grave even though everyone had so many expectations.

But after all, a door is just a door which can be opened or closed. It can be blocked or passed through and it can be an ending or a beginning. The infinity hidden behind it might arouse your enormous imagination and make you willingly get engaged in another round of exerting efforts, so in this sense to say "there is nothing" is not right, because there is a "door," then behind it there could be "everything."

And a good novel is like this: starting at one door and ending at another.

II.

A hard-working salesman who has the responsibility of supporting the family woke up one morning and found himself becoming a large beetle. If you hold your breath, you might see a small crystal ball under a floor in a house in a city one moment, and your previous moments and current moments, as well as the mankind's past, present, and future, are all collected inside it. There is such a book that each page of it will disappear immediately after you read it, never to be found again. A teenager, to take his revenge for his father being killed, had his own head cut off into a pot of boiling water to struggle with his enemy's head brutally...

Are these novel plots or dreams? Perhaps it's hard to distinguish. This is not a real world but a possible one. It has the characteristics of flying to the vast sky and the divinity beyond. It's just like a tree, which roots in reality's mediocrity, absurdness, and hardships, and extends its branches of desire and beauty to the sky. In my mind, a good novel should be like this: it has its own air, river, sunshine, four seasons, and day and night. Maybe its world is totally different from the world you live in, but it can truly reflect your dream of beauty, and your real understanding of a possible world. In such a world, there is only boundary to imagination, and boundary to the depth and width of a writer's heart, but there is no boundary to whether something is true or not.

So in this sense, for me, writing and dreaming are the same thing.

Many years ago, I once wrote a casual poem:

Life is so hard, if without dream;
Dream is walking on a single-plank bridge; while
we walk on dream;

Under white mist and fog, where is the preexistence, future, and afterlife?
There is a lighthouse far, far away, to erect for the blind;
If dream drops suddenly, numerous hearts will be splashed.

No matter how many transient joys we have in life, death will surely come to wipe it out or throw it into the shade, so our life is just like a prisoner's short road to execution, and it is the only road that can't be changed or be repeated or be chosen again, which means we are doomed to only see the scenery on this road, so the only way to make up is to dream. We are doomed to die and we can live only once, while dreaming can let us enjoy life many times. In dreams we can see the scenes we can't see in our life, and we can walk in other directions the prisoner can't walk.

Dreams are often visionary and fleeting, but when they are recorded by words, they become another reality which will not disappear easily. And through writing we can better know ourselves and the world, and extract some unexpected and beautiful things from the depths of our body sunk in sleep. Writing makes our life; the world as well as inevitable death become endurable, and through it we capture our time, the world, and ourselves. In this sense, I think this well-known saying might be expressed in reverse order: life is gray, but the tree of dream can be evergreen.

—December 11, 2008, Beijing

Another Scenery

Between Guo Suping and Zhong Jingjing

Guo Suping (hereinafter referred as "Guo"): Most of the narratives of the new generation of writers are quite close to life and reality, while the art world of your novel lets us taste another way of thinking and of narrative, another emotion field, and another aesthetic orientation of young writers, and your style adds a new beautiful landscape to the overall pattern of new generation's creation, so I think we can name out conservation as "another scenery."

Zhong Jingjing (hereinafter referred as "Zhong"): OK. The name is nice.

Guo: From most of your early works, such as *Gardenia in the Rain* and *War Nursery Rhymes*, my most distinct impression is the dream world and absurdity of those story plots, and with them you long for the brightness of human nature and feeling which is almost impossible to exist in reality, and you also exploit and castigate the social dark corners. And with the development of stories, the characters surpass the boundary of life and death and they can freely go into and come out of the two worlds. They seem absurd but they still make sense; they are beyond anticipation but still logical and reasonable. I think maybe this is because you don't just indulge in the narrative of stories, while the exploration of humans' deep psychological and emotional world is the essence of your works; or in other words, stories are just external appearance, a kind of carrier of expression and hope. It is through the support of this potential meaning that the works leave us memorable and thoughtful space. So please tell us why you choose to use such a narrative way for your writing.

Zhong: Because I think the dream is another kind of reality, another kind of existence which we just can't touch, but this doesn't mean it is unreasonable or absurd or nonexistent. The actual world should contain many things. Its scope is very broad. One kind of life is appreciable daily life, while the other kind is just a human's imagination, memory, and dream world, and what is included in dreams, memories, and imagination is quite comprehensive, far beyond the real world. It keeps humans' memories of feelings and experiences in real life, but also the memories of human ancestors in remote times, just as I wrote in *Crossroads*. Therefore, I think man's soul is larger than reality, and the purpose of writing is to surpass the reality instead of copying it. The greatest writers are those who create their own worlds. Instead of telling others what the world looks like, writers should tell those things beyond the world, and give the world another meaning as well as a brand new logic to interpret it.

Guo: Speaking of dreams, you already wrote *You Can't Understand My Dream* in 2001, which gave dreams a straight analysis, but I find what you wrote recently is different from the past, for in the past you focused on the reality in dreams while now you are focusing on the dream world in real life. Besides, dreams are only your manifestations, while your real concern is human psychology, which directly explores and dissects the most secret and darkest place of human nature.

Zhong: Yes, at first the dream world appears numinous or unnatural, but indeed it is quite realistic and true; while on the contrary, a human's daily behaviors have much guise and concealment. Being a special reality, dream life is an important part of human life. Reality and dream are the two sides of human life, one inside and the other outside, and it's not enough if we only write the daily life without the dream. Dreams are very mysterious, and though you never experience them in your real life, this combination, experience, and memory all have some kind of superpower.

Guo: You are not a soldier, but your early works that aroused the literary circle's attention and praise are about wars, such as *War Nursery Rhymes*, and the subject of war accounts for a large proportion of your early writing. They have the magic flavor of your characteristics, but they don't have the smell of gunpowder, and sometimes their back-grounds are a little vague, such as the works *War Nursery Rhymes*, "Letters from Qiliang," and "Bunker," which makes us feel wars are just a kind of atmosphere that is proper for the development of narrative. So is it your writing strategy to dilute it on purpose?

Zhong: I am not a soldier, so it's impossible for me to write the real life of a contemporary army, and I can only write the abstract war which dilutes its historical background. In this case, when I wrote such a war without opposing sides or spe-cific historical background, I was writing the persons under an unusual situation, especially a kind of pure humanity. I think the war theme is actually a very good one, because un-der such an unusual situation as war, death is clearly in sight and touchable. As a result, a person's choices and actions become more startling, and everything from human nature, including kindness, evil, beauty, ugliness, bravery, sadness, greatness, and nobleness, can be thoroughly described to the extreme.

Guo: Such a flavor in your recent works! *Empty Grave* is particularly strong, and your exploration of human nature becomes deeper and more complicated. Although this work is about revolutionary history instead of war, its history has become a stage where human nature can be richly displayed. On and off the stage, various kinds of human tragedies, com-edies, and even farces are racing to be shown, but after all the flowers fall, what we see is a shocking blankness. The pre-vious symphony-like arrangement and the final pause-style ending form a huge force to fully highlight its theme. How do you have such an originality of ideas?

Zhong: To be honest, I don't think there is any originality in it. It was not sought deliberately, but was picked easily from my early years working at collecting materials of revo-lutionary history and the history of the Chinese Communist Party. When this novel was reprinted, I wrote an essay on its creation whose title was "Another Kind of History." Yes, what I wrote was the real history I gained during my interview but was neglected on purpose by our textbooks and our official history compilers. They were buried under those towering monuments for big heroes and events, and they were silent but incomparably real, just like the land and weeds both barren and fertile, both dull and complicated. Too many things had to be filtered out when a person was written to be a hero by us. The theme of this novel relates to the relationships between revolutionaries and ordinary people; between rebels and their families; and between saving and holding fast, all of which are fascinating subjects for me, and I touched on them in my previous works such as "Jingzi" and *Rescue*, while in the novel they have more lively and real stories to support. This novel should be written better.

Guo: Speaking of writing history, I noticed that more and more of your works in recent years turned to real history from dreams and fantasy. And in your reconstruction of history, the profound reality metaphor and humanistic concern can be easily found. Furthermore, they became more thorough and harmonious, such as *Empty Tomb*, which is about revolutionary history; *Family History*, which is family history; and *Story of Huangyangbao*, which is about childhood memory. They put forward a profound question to human nature from the point of family relationships, while in the past about similar themes we feel more condemnation of the situation. But without actual situations we can't recognize human nature's darkness, which was disclosed through the story of Peter in the Bible. The more important thing is that we should have a repentant heart, which is lacking in our national character. So from this perspective, your works are really of great value, because this is a big stride from reflection on the situation to human's introspection. How did you accomplish this?

Zhong: Here involves a word—guilt. You are right that our nation lacks a guilty conscience and a repentant heart, and as a result, though we suffered a lot of hardships we haven't surpassed ourselves yet. Speaking of introspection, there were such kinds of works in early history, such as the Bible.

In the Bible, Pilate, the governor, at first did have compassion toward Jesus. At that time, two prisoners would be put to death: one was Jesus and the other was Barabbas, a murderer. According to custom, one of them could be amnestied, but when Pilate asked the crowd to make the choice, the crowd chose the murderer and decided to let Jesus be put to death. Pilate couldn't understand, and asked them, "Why? What crime has he committed?" The crowd didn't answer him, but just shouted, "Crucify him!" To be frank, I don't think this is just a story that happened in the Bible or in history 2,000 years ago; I think it happens now and it is a common thing. The story in *Family History* is true, and it's just what happened in our family in the past several decades, which is by no means unique to our family, and I am sure that many Chinese families have experienced it. History was created by both the victims and the victimizers together, and are the victims really so innocent? Perhaps such a question is a little too cruel, so I think guilt is a kind of fate, and the so-called "unbearable heaviness of being" is just this meaning.

Guo: In your works, there are a lot of descriptions of memories about suffering, such as in *The Third Person*, and besides showing man's struggle and repentance, they also contain a huge compassion through the revelation of darkness in reality and human nature and thus bring about a different kind of aesthetic significance. I think such a kind of writing technique is inseparable from your philosophy of life and art ideas.

Zhong: Actually, my view of the world and life is quite pessimistic. I think suffering is more a fate than something you can struggle with, and none of us can escape it. Because of such an understanding, I think a good work should start from sadness and then sublimate to beauty, just like a flower blooming in the mire of misery; though its root is painful, its flower is beautiful and quiet. It should go beyond the judgment of the good and evil in a moral sense, and go beyond anger and condemnation to embody a kind of realization and pity to suffering. Where is the meaning of a great tragedy? It is not in the description of how sad and miserable the reality is, but in the expression of how people struggle and survive when facing sadness and misery. And during the struggle, the spirit of beauty rises, which, in my opinion, has the force to support people to survive, and which is also what a writer should display. In this sense, beauty and sadness are connected to each other and interdependent. I even think sadness is the indispensable essence and reason of beauty.

Guo: What kind of relationship do you think a writer should keep with reality?

Zhong: A person's choice of writing is indeed a choice of a kind of lifestyle. When a writer is so acceptable to reality and he feels enjoyable, it's not possible for his works to have much power of transcendence and criticism. The writer Yu Hua once said that he had a kind of strained relationship with reality, and I think many writers have the same feeling, while writing is just a way to escape or to break out from such tension or oppression. Only when you feel sad or disappointed in this world will you try to seek another kind of world. For me, writing is just like this. Just as what I said in "Writing and Dreaming," I take writing as a way to record my dreams. We are destined to die, and the life of everybody is just like the short distance for a prisoner on death row on his way to be executed. Since this is the only way, we can only enjoy the scenery on the way, while dreams can bring us various sceneries and this means we can live our lives many times. Besides, writing is like a big piece of glass to separate me from the real world, and I can stand inside it to face the world. I can choose not to look at it, and I can even make faces at it.

Guo: Because of this, it is very important for a writer to pursue the beauty of originality and to question reality. Without the reference of imagination, the world will become inconceivable. So in this sense, your works surpass reality instead of separating from it.

Zhong: This is the direction of my efforts. To surpass means to give my own world my own logic first and then open the reader's field of vision. The purpose of novels is to discover, just as Kafka said, that a good work is like a sharp axe that can cut open the frozen world in your heart, which means novels must open a new vision.

Zhong Jingjing's Creation Chronological Table

In 1996, historical novel *The Kunyang Blood Riding*, published by PLA Literature and Art Publishing House.

In 1997, collection of short stories, *War Nursery Rhymes*, published in No. 2 of *PLA Literature and Art*, and won the PLA Literature and Art Award of year 1997–1998.

Short story "Jingzi" published in No. 2 of *Harvest*.

In 1998, novel *There is a Cat on the Roof* published in No. 2 of *Chinese Writer*.

Novel *Noontime's Attitude* published in No. 9 of *Shanghai Literature*.

Short story "Gardenia in the Rain" published in No. 2 of *Yan River*.

Short story "Libation Ridge" published in No. 2 of *Yan River*.

Short story "Calling for Help at Midnight" published in No. 2 of *Yan River*.

In 1999, short story "Porcelain Doll" published in No. 2 of *Southwest Military Literature and Art*.

Short story "Moluo Flowers" and short story "Letters from Qiliang" published in No. 5 of *PLA Literature and Art*.

Short story "Past Events" published in No. 6 of *Shandong Literature*.

In 2000, novel *Li Tomb* published by PLA Literature and Art Publishing House.

Short novel *Crossroads* and short story "Winter Days" published in No. 1 of *Shanghai Literature*.

In 2001, novel *Story of Huangyangbao* published by Changjiang Literature and Art Publishing House.

Collection of short stories *War Nursery Rhymes* published by Changjiang Literature and Art Publishing House.

Novel *Rescue* published in No. 6 of *Harvest*.

Novel *Stories of Xiling* published in No. 5 of *Zhongshan*.

Novel *The Son of Tribulus* published in No. 10 of *People's Literature*.

Short story "The Hand of Grandma" and short story "Bunker" published in No. 6 of *Yan River*.

In 2002, novel *You Can't Understand My Dream* published in No. 5 of *Harvest*.

Novel *Cat Season* published in No. 5 of *Great Wall*.

In 2004, novel *Empty Grave* published in No. 5 of *Great Wall*.

Novel *Purple: Stories At and Out of the Window* published in No. 5 of *Yan River*.

Short story "The Appointment of 1938" published in No. 5 of *Fiction Forest*.

In 2005, novel *Family History* published in No. 2 of *People's Literature*.

Novel *The Third Person* published in No. 3 of *Flower City*.

Short story "Distant Tashi" published in No. 8 of *Yan River*.

Novel *Valley* published in No. 8 of *Red Bean*.

Novel *Days of Sparrows* published in No. 10 of *Ethnic Literature*.

Novel *My Left Hand* published in No. 5 of *October*.

In 2006, collection of novels *You Can't Understand My Dream* published by Chunfeng Literature and Art Publishing House.

Novel *Who Took My Index Finger* published in No. 7 of *Beijing Literature*.

Novel *Osmanthus Rain* published in No. 6 of *Great Wall*.

Short story "Empty San" published in No. 4 of *Olive Green*.

In 2007, novel *Red Bird* published in No. 1 of *Grain in Ear*.

Novel *Crying Box* published in No. 4 of *Novel Monthly* (original edition).

Novel *A Small Basket Floating by My House* published in No. 7 of *Chinese Writer*.

In 2008, novel *Kunyang* published by Flower City Publishing House.

Novel *Li Tomb* published by Flower City Publishing House.

Novel *Moonlight at Fifteen* published in No. 1 of *Bulaohu Novel*.

Short story "The Husband in Dream" published in No. 5 of *Urban Fiction*.

Short story "Night Buses" published in No. 7 of *Shanghai Literature*.

Short story "Case Narrative" published in No. 8 of *Guangzhou Literature and Art*.

In 2009, novel *Hand Lines* published in No. 8 of *October*.

CPSIA information can be obtained
at www.ICGtesting.com
Printed in the USA
LVOW11s1815300517

536306LV00002B/403/P